99% Faking It

Sweet Snarky Romance Series, Volume 4

Chris Cannon

Published by CC Publishing, 2024.

Edited by Erin Molta
Cover design by Chris Canada
Cover art by Canva
ISBN: 9781964956152
First Edition March 2019
Second Edition July 2024

Also by Chris Cannon

Going Down In Flames
Bridges Burned
Trial By Fire
Fanning The Flames
Burning Bright

Mysteries of Mystic Hills
Murder in Mystic Hills
Double Trouble in Mystic Hills
SpellBound in Mystic Hills

Sweet Snarky Romance Series
The Boyfriend Bet
Boomerang Boyfriend
The Dating Debate
99% Faking It

Watch for more at https://www.chriscannonauthor.com/.

Chapter One

Lisa

Matt walked toward me with an easy grin on his face. He'd finally started to relax around me now that he realized I wasn't going to throw myself at him. Not that I hadn't entertained the idea, because he had chocolate-brown eyes and dark wavy hair and broad shoulders and...wait...*where am I going with this?*

Right. I wasn't throwing myself at man-candy-Matt because he'd made it clear that he thought of me only as a friend. And at first that had sort of sucked, but I was a big girl and I could deal with it. He made a good friend. We had fun together.

At one time, I may have held out hope that he would turn to me and say, "Lisa, I was wrong. You're exactly the short, nerdy girl I've been looking for." But it had been a few months and now I was over it. At this point in my life I wasn't sure any guy was worth the trouble. Until some new guy showed up and took my breath away, I was declaring my life a drama-free, date-free zone.

Matt sat down next to me at our normal lunch table in the Greenbrier High School cafeteria and opened his brown paper bag. "Are you and Nina getting your nerd on tonight?" he asked.

"Is it Friday?" I said, like it answered the question, because it totally did. Every Friday night my best friend Nina and I engaged in Nerd-girl Festivities. We went to Books-A-Million to find new treasures and then hung out in the coffee shop afterward talking books and boys and anything else that came to mind. "What about you?" I asked. "Any exciting plans?"

He shrugged. "Not sure yet."

"Someone has commitment issues," I teased in a sing- song voice.

"Hey," Matt said, "I'm just a guy who likes to keep his options open."

"Please. You have a pathological resistance about committing to plans. You always wait until the last second." "Right." Matt took a bite of his sandwich.

"Just because your mom's a therapist doesn't mean you're qualified to analyze me."

"My mom's job doesn't have anything to do with it." I popped the top on my soda and took a drink. "I've seen you try to pick out a donut at Krispy Kreme."

"It's not my fault they all look good."

"Yes, but most people have a favorite." Maybe that was his problem with dating. All girls looked good and he couldn't pick one. "Let's try an exercise my mom does with her clients. If you could do anything tonight, no matter how impractical, what would you choose?"

Matt's gaze flicked over to the table where his younger sister sat with her best friend Jane and then he glanced back at me. "That's a stupid question."

Busted. I leaned in so no one would overhear us. "I didn't ask *who* you'd do."

"What's that supposed to mean?" Matt's tone was a little too defensive.

"Nothing." Jane had a steady boyfriend, who happened to be drop-dead gorgeous, and they appeared to be very much in love. That didn't stop Matt from staring at her whenever he thought no one was looking. Since I used to spend a fair amount of my time checking out Matt while he was otherwise occupied, I recognized the game he was playing. It was a no-win situation.

...

Nina picked me up to go to the bookstore a few hours after school. "So you and Matt seemed awful chatty at lunch today. Anything I should know about?"

"Nope. I'm still living my life in the friend zone." I tilted the air-conditioning vents down so the air didn't hit me in the face. Short girl problem 101. Whatever normal-sized person who'd sat here last had left the vents aimed so the air blew my hair all around my face. Since I wasn't modeling for a shampoo commercial, this was not an ideal setting.

"I know you still like him," Nina said. "Wrong. That ship has sailed."

"Are you sure? West said Matt talks about you when
you're not around."

I froze for a second and then took a cleansing breath. "Please tell me you're not discussing my past crush with your boyfriend. That would be in direct violation of the best friend code."

"Wrong. It doesn't count if he's the one that asked about you. He said Matt talks about you almost as much as he talks about Jane."

"Does he realize Matt is into Jane?"

"I don't think so and the better question is why does Matt have a crush on a girl who is obviously so into her boyfriend? And no offense, but not many people could compete with that guy."

"It's kind of karma that she isn't into him," I said. "He'll just have to move on, like I did."

"Fine. If you've moved on, then who are you interested in?"

"No one, for the moment," I said. "Although I'm actively looking for a new book boyfriend. Hopefully, I'll find a fabulous new guy at the bookstore."

"This is totally selfish, but you need a real boyfriend so we can double-date."

I laughed. "So my love life should revolve around yours? Is that what you're saying?"

"Yes," Nina said. "And I'd appreciate it if you'd get with the program."

"I'll get right on that." I knew she was joking but part of it rang true and that kind of bothered me. Is this what life was going to be like from now on? If my best friend has a boyfriend I'd better find one, too, or soon I wouldn't have a best friend anymore? Because that would suck.

"Hey," Nina said. "You know I'm joking, right?"

"I know." I sighed and slid lower in my seat. "I have to tell you I don't have a lot of trust in the male half of the species." Given that my mom was a family counselor, it was the irony of ironies that my dad had abandoned her when she'd told him she was pregnant. They'd been married less than a year, and I guess the idea of being a parent had freaked him out.

My mom said one day she came home from work and he was gone. No discussion. No warning. Just a bunch of empty drawers and a note about how he wasn't ready to be a father. She'd received divorce papers in the mail before I was even born. I'd never even met the guy and pretty much thought of him as nothing more than a sperm donor and a complete douchebag.

"Given your situation, that's justified. But look at your mom now. She's been dating the same guy for years."

"Yeah, Tony is great," I said. "But I don't think it's a coincidence that they've never even discussed marriage."

"Maybe he has his own reasons for not wanting to get married," Nina said.

"It's weird. I've overheard his cell calls to an insurance company about some woman's bills and prescriptions. I'm kind of afraid of what that might mean."

"Okay. So either he's cheating on his sick wife, or he's stayed married to someone he doesn't love so his insurance will cover her medical bills?" Nina pulled into the lot of the bookstore and parked in the front row. "That's either terrible or tragic."

"I've almost asked my mom about it a few times, but if she's okay with the situation then it can't be too shady." Everything my mom did was above board. Her motto was *Honesty is the best and only policy.* "Maybe it's his sister or his mom or something." I unbuckled my seatbelt. "I'm done with all this stressful real life crap. I'm ready to get my happily ever after on. Let's go buy some books."

We entered the bookstore. I inhaled the scent of coffee and ink-covered pages, my two favorite fragrances, and suddenly all was Zen in my world. A new display of Harry Potter shirts and bags caught my eye and sucked me in like a tractor beam.

I ran my fingers down the strap of a messenger bag with an owl pattern on one side and Platform 9 ¾ on the other. It seemed to be calling my name. I opened the flap. The bag was divided into two compartments and even had loops for pens. "I love this."

"It's cute," Nina said. "I don't really need another bag." "Since when does *need* have anything to do with it?" I had what some might call a purse problem. I liked to think of it as an eclectic collection of geek-girl handbags.

"Didn't you tell me not to let you buy any more purses?"

I hugged the messenger bag to my chest. "I have no recollection of that conversation."

"Do you have room in your closet for another purse?"

I pictured the shelf in the top of my closet. My handbags were lined up facing out like they were on display because seeing them made me happy. There wasn't much room left. "If I put the Darth Vader bag inside the Tardis bag I could fit this one up there, too."

"I would point out that the Darth Vader bag is bigger than the Tardis," Nina said. "But I know what your response to that statement would be."

"It's bigger on the inside." I grinned. While Nina didn't share a love for all my geeky fandoms, she did at least understand and appreciate them. I ran my hand over the bag. "But cross pollinating fandoms might lead to a disruption in the space-time continuum, so I could just keep this bag on my dresser."

Nina snorted but didn't bother responding. Then she picked up a pair of socks with an owl and wand pattern. "You can never have too many pairs of socks and they take up much less room."

I sighed and checked the price on the bag. It was more than I wanted to spend. So, I reluctantly set it back down. "Don't worry, dear. I'll be watching for you to go on clearance." I grabbed a pair of socks decorated with the Sorting Hat and Harry Potter spectacles and checked the price tag. "These are cute and much more budget friendly."

My job at Crazy Crafts kept me in yarn and books with a little left over for fun money. I crocheted scarves and sold them on Etsy, so in a way one of my hobbies paid for itself.

Now that we were headed into warmer weather, my scarf sales would drop. That was okay. I could crochet and stock up for next winter.

"Good choice. I declare tomorrow Harry Potter sock day," Nina stated like it was a new holiday.

"Works for me."

Chapter Two

Matt

Lisa wasn't wrong about me waiting to make plans until the last minute. It wasn't because I couldn't commit, it was because I liked keeping my options open. West would make plans for us, and I could sit back and chill out. Why work when someone else would take care of it? *Work smarter, not harder* was a motto for a reason.

Not that I was afraid of hard work. I worked with my dad in our family landscaping business. I could dig up old hedges and shovel mulch all day, as long as I was outside breathing fresh air. When it came down to it, I wasn't a people person. I mean I liked some people, but loud, crowded places weren't my favorite.

I checked the kitchen clock. Jane was coming to pick up my sister Haley soon. I wasn't going to fall all over myself staring at her, but I wanted to say hello. A few months ago,

I would have made sure to wait for Jane on the porch swing so I could intercept her before she came into the house and talk to her while Haley was getting ready. I was done playing that game, which is why I was in the kitchen warming up a hot pocket when Jane knocked on the door. It's not like I had some sort of radar that let me know when she was close. I saw her walking up the front porch through the picture window.

"Come in," I hollered.

She opened the door. "Hey, Matt."

"Hey." It was best to keep conversation to a minimum. "Haley's up in her room."

"I could have guessed that." Jane headed up the stairs as my fraternal twin brother Charlie came down. They nodded at each other and then he joined me in the kitchen. My phone vibrated with a text. I checked the message. "West says he's meeting us at Clarissa's."

"That's the plan."

"Cool." Charlie's girlfriend had a big backyard, which was perfect for barbecues. Even if there were a lot of people, it would be outside, which was better than being crowded into someone's living room or basement.

...

Once we reached Clarissa's, I found a lawn chair on the far side of the patio and surveyed my options. There were half a dozen couples and a few single girls. No one I was interested in. Too bad Lisa was off doing nerd-girl activities. She was always fun to hang out with.

West showed up and sat by me. "So how much fun are we having tonight?" he asked.

"I think you should text Nina and tell her we're at a Harry Potter party and that chick who played Hermione is here, and she wants to meet them."

He grinned. "Yeah, that would get them out here." "Seriously," I said. "How long can they look at books?"

"For hours. Thank God they have a cafe in the bookstore. I've learned to go grab a coffee and wait while I read on my phone."

"You read on your phone at the bookstore...where they sell books?"

"You've seen my house," West said. "Right. Sorry."

West's mom was a hoarder. They'd tried to find her help. She'd seen several therapists, but that didn't stop her from filling their house from floor to ceiling with random junk. West's dad was OCD, so he organized all the crap in plastic tubs. Sometimes I wondered how West kept it together.

Two blondes came toward us. "Hey, West," blonde number one said.

"Hey," he responded.

"Are you still dating your neighbor?" she asked. He nodded.

"Too bad." She giggled and walked on by. Blonde number two's cheeks were red. As she walked past me, she said, "Being a wingman can be embarrassing."

I grinned and nodded. She smiled and kept on walking. "Go talk to her," West said.

I shook my head. She was cute but I wasn't interested. "Why not?" he asked.

Time to change the subject. "Is it my imagination or do more girls flirt with you now that you have a girlfriend?" "Seems like it."

Charlie and Clarissa came toward us with a guy I'd never seen before. He definitely wasn't from around here. He looked like he thought he was trying out for the role of a rock star or a rebel in a movie. His hair was short on the sides and long on top so it flipped over and almost hid one of his eyes. His ripped jeans screamed, *I'm trying too hard.*

"Hey guys," Clarissa said, "this is my cousin Trey." I held out my hand. "I'm Matt."

Trey shook my hand. "Charlie's twin brother."

I nodded. "And this is West." They shook hands.

"Trey just moved here," Clarissa said. "He's a little obnoxious, but once you get past his hair, he's okay."

Trey laughed. "You wish your hair was as cool as mine." "Right," Clarissa said.

"Please tell me this isn't all there is to do in this town." Trey gestured at the patio and everyone sitting around it.

"If you're looking for excitement, you came to the wrong place," I answered.

"I was afraid you were going to say that."

"What are you talking about?" Clarissa said. "You can go see a movie, go out to eat, hang out at barbecues, or go play golf at the country club."

"Do I look like I golf?" Trey asked, like he was disgusted by the idea.

I laughed. Maybe this guy wasn't so bad. The smell of hotdogs drifted through the air.

"I can't believe I'm about to say this," Trey said. "But those hot dogs smell awesome."

"Watch out," Clarissa said. "You wouldn't want anyone to think you liked being here."

"Don't worry," Trey said. "I'll scowl while I eat." They headed over to the grill.

"Do you want to go grab a pizza?" West asked. "Because I had hot dogs for dinner almost every night this week."

I knew his mom didn't cook, but that was sad. "Sure."

The Slicery was crowded, but we only had to wait about ten minutes for a table. We were halfway through our sausage and pepperoni thick-crust pizza with extra cheese when Nina and Lisa walked in the door.

Nina spotted us and headed over with a big smile for West. Lisa followed along behind her like she knew the situation was inevitable.

"Did you know we were coming here?" Nina asked as she sat down next to him.

"No," West said. "I was trying to avoid hot dogs."

Lisa sat in the chair beside me. "So, what did you guys do tonight?"

"Barbecue...it was kind of boring," I said.

"You should have come to the bookstore," Lisa said with complete sincerity.

"Because it's never boring at the bookstore?" I asked.

"Nope." She shook her head. "Never."

The waitress came over and asked if they needed a menu.

"No," Lisa said, "I want iced tea with lemon and a small meatball pizza."

"Meatballs on a pizza?" I said. "That's just wrong."

"Pizza is Italian," she countered. "Meatballs are Italian. How can that be wrong?"

"Meatballs go on spaghetti," I pointed out. "Not on pizza crust."

"You're wrong." She grinned. "Then again, you're probably used to being in that position, so who am I to argue?"

"Hey, Miss Overachiever, I may not always know the answer but that doesn't mean I'm wrong."

She squinted at me. "There's the right answer and then there is the one that is the opposite of right. Wait...what do they call that? I know...wrong."

"Not caring about the questions doesn't make me wrong. It just means that it's a game I don't want to play."

"So you're opting out. That's kind of lazy."

I cracked my knuckles. "I like to think of it as conserving energy."

"I'm pretty sure that's another word for lazy," Lisa teased.

"Nope. I just conserve my effort and spend energy on things that are important to me."

"How short is that list?" she asked.

"Pretty short," I admitted.

"Am I on it?" She batted her eyelashes at me, which made me smile.

"There is a section for book-loving, nerd-girl friends, so yeah you have a spot."

"I'm honored."

When her pizza arrived, it looked good and smelled amazing.

"You want to try a piece, don't you?" Lisa grabbed a slice and dropped it on my plate.

"Since you put it on my plate, I wouldn't want to waste food." I picked it up and took a bite. It was better than spaghetti and meatballs. "I may have to admit I was wrong about this."

She grinned. "If you follow my lead, everything will work out in your favor."

Chapter Three

Lisa

The alarm went off on my cell. *Noooooo.* It couldn't be morning already. Where had Saturday and Sunday gone? I needed a rewind button. I was not emotionally prepared to deal with Monday. Maybe if I ignored it, it would go away. I hit snooze and rolled over.

"Lisa, you need to wake up," my mom called out from the other room.

"I don't want to," I hollered back.

"I know what will get you out of bed." I heard the microwave door open and close and then the hum of something cooking. The smell of bacon drifted into my room.

"That's not fair," I called out.

"You better get your butt in here before I eat it all." Bacon was my kryptonite. It was the only thing that would get me up and moving some mornings. I threw back my Tardis bedspread and stumbled into the kitchen. Three pieces of bacon and two slices of wheat toast waited for me on the table.

"Thank you." I sat down and bit into a piece of salty crispy goodness. Yum.

"You're welcome." She adjusted a bobby pin in the messy bun she wrangled her curly brown hair into. "I swear sometimes it feels like these things are trying to burrow into my head."

"What's with the dress?" Normally she wore low-key flowy skirts and blouses but this dress was tailored and made out of stiff material like a suit.

"In a moment of insanity, I decided I should try to look more like an adult."

"You mean uncomfortable and crabby?" I asked.

"Pretty much. Remind me to burn this dress when I come home. I have to go. I have an early appointment."

"See you tonight." I finished my breakfast and fantasized about crawling back into bed. Why had I stayed up until one thirty to finish my book? It had seemed like a good idea at the time. Now...not so much.

13

After taking a too-long shower, I did minimal hair and makeup. I was just going to school. Not like I was trying to impress anyone. I threw on a black sweatshirt which said "Siriusly?" and my favorite comfortable jeans. Where were my black Keds? I checked in the living room, behind the bathroom door, and under my bed. Nope.

"*Accio* Keds," I said and waited for a split second to see if it might possibly work. Nope. Still a Muggle. Damn it.

I dug out a pair of black booties that laced up like

combat boots. Thank goodness there was a zipper on the side because I didn't want to unlace those suckers every time I took them on and off. The only problem with the boots was now my fun new Harry Potter socks wouldn't show. Whatever. I checked my cell. I needed to get my butt out the door if I didn't want to be late.

Because life seemed to have a strange sense of humor, I hit every red light on the way. Half a block from school, I was about to drive through an intersection on a green light when some old man and his poodle decided it was a good time to cross the road. I slammed on my brakes and prayed the guy behind me was paying attention. I heard brakes squealing and horns honking. When I checked my rearview mirror, the guy behind me was shaking his fist at me. Like this was my fault. Jerk. Once the dog and his owner were out of the street, I accelerated more slowly than I needed to, just to give the guy behind me some grief because, in my opinion, sometimes karma needed a little help. The guy took a right turn and I went back up to normal speed.

I pulled into the Greenbrier High School parking lot and found a halfway decent spot. Maybe everyone was running a little late this morning. After turning the car off, I sat there for a moment. I didn't have any tests today. My homework was done. I could do this, but that didn't mean I was happy about it.

"Monday mornings suck," I announced to the world as I climbed out of my car.

"We might be soul mates," a masculine voice said from behind me.

I turned to see a guy with cool hair, ripped jeans, and a black leather jacket striding toward me. And suddenly my morning didn't seem so bad. I smiled at him. "You're new."

"The hair gave me away, didn't it?" He grinned. "I'm Trey."

"Lisa," I said.

"Here's a test to see how small this town really is. If I said I'm Clarissa's cousin, do you know who I'm talking about?"

"Does your cousin date Charlie Patterson?" I asked as we walked toward the main entrance.

"Damn." He reached up and ran his fingers through his hair, brushing it back off of his face. "It's worse than I thought."

"Greenbrier isn't that small but my best friend Nina dates Charlie's cousin."

"Should I give in and go buy a flannel shirt right now?" he asked.

We did wear a lot of flannel at this time of year. Our town wasn't exactly a fashion capital.

"Maybe," I said. "But it's not that bad. There are three hundred people in the senior class and about twelve hundred total in the school."

"Could be worse, I guess."

"Where did you move from?"

"Just outside of Chicago. My high school had twice as many people," he said. "And zero to no flannel."

I was suddenly glad I hadn't put on a flannel shirt this morning. "We're halfway through March, so flannel weather should be over soon."

"Good to know." We climbed the steps to the front door. "Which way is the main office?"

I pointed to the right. "Straight that way."

"Thanks, Lisa. I'll see you around."

"See you." I watched him walk away. He was cute and funny and could hold a conversation. Maybe I'd found someone who was worth the drama.

Matt, West, and Nina were already sitting at our lunch table by the time I made it there. The cafeteria smelled like sloppy joes. I was pretty sure the red stuff on the meat that wasn't real hamburger wasn't really barbecue sauce, so I stuck with my standard peanut butter and jelly. "So, I met Clarissa's cousin," I said to Nina.

"The guy with the cool hair?" she asked.

I nodded.

Matt snorted.

"Do you have an opinion you'd like to share with the class?" I asked.

"He's trying too hard," Matt said.

At least he was putting forth some sort of effort. I didn't say that out loud because I doubt Matt would appreciate it. It's not like he was a slob, but he didn't seem to care about clothes. Then again, he looked like the poster boy for the broad-shouldered, all-American guy next door no matter what he wore. "Where'd you meet Trey?"

"At Clarissa's barbecue." He leaned toward me. "Here's a question for your therapist mom. Why do more girls flirt with West now that he has a girlfriend?"

"Sounds like the wedding ring effect. The theory is that a woman in a bar wearing a ring will get hit on more than a woman without one. Must be some perverse sense of human nature to want what you can't have."

Trey walked into the lunch room, talking to a girl from the acting club. She had multiple piercings in her ears and was a master of winged eyeliner. "Do you think I should wear more makeup?"

"Why?" Matt asked.

"I was thinking about trying a new look."

Matt's gaze tracked mine. "Because of him?"

"Maybe," I said. "Or maybe his cool hair made me realize I don't have to look like every other girl in this school if I don't want to."

"We could go to the mall and do makeovers," Nina said.

"Sounds like fun."

• • •

That night I drove Nina to the mall with a mission on my mind: find a new look I liked for myself that might attract Trey's attention.

"So why are we really doing this?" Nina asked.

"Multiple reasons," I said. "It's my senior year. I've been wearing the same pink lip gloss and mascara for two years. I'm ready for a change."

"Your mom would tell you not to change your look for a guy," Nina reminded me.

"I've been rocking the low-maintenance nerd-girl look for years. Maybe I want to try something else. And Trey might notice me, but if he doesn't, that's okay."

At the mall, the girl behind the counter was more than happy to try and sell me hot pink eyeliner. Not going to happen. "How about something more normal...like blue."

She pulled out several shades of blue. "This navy would make your brown eyes really pop."

"Sounds painful," I said.

"What?"

Apparently sarcasm wasn't her thing. "Never mind.

Let's try the navy."

I let her apply the eyeliner on my left eye and watched how she did it. Then I repeated the process on my right eye. The two weren't a perfect match, but I didn't do too bad. The color did make my brown eyes stand out in an I'm-not-trying-too-hard kind of way.

"We have the matching lipstick," the girl said.

"Blue lipstick?" Nina said like she might have misunderstood.

"It's really popular," the makeup expert said, like she truly believed it.

"I'll stick with gloss...something darker than pale pink," I said.

She pulled out a burgundy tube that sparkled. I accepted the sample applicator she loaded up and handed to me. I swiped it across my lips, checked the mirror, and... Nope. "How about a color that doesn't make me look like a vampire recently drained all the blood from my body?"

"Yeah, that one definitely isn't for you. Wipe it off." She handed me a cotton ball doused in makeup remover. "And I'll find one that will work better for your skin tone."

I swiped the cotton ball across my lips and *yuck*. It felt slimy and smelled like flowers. I grabbed a tissue and scrubbed at my lips. "That was gross."

The girl frowned and looked at the pump bottle she'd used to douse the cotton ball. "Sorry, that's the moisturizer, not the makeup remover."

I was beginning to doubt this woman's expertise. She must have seen the look on my face. "Sorry. They changed all the packaging and I'm still figuring out what's what. This gloss should work for you." She held up a hot pink tube that shimmered.

It appeared to be a more exciting version of the one I already had. I swiped it on. Still me, but amped up a bit for fun.

"You look good," Nina confirmed.

"We have a winner."

Nina went next, trying on a few glosses before picking one out. She passed on the eye liner. "I'm good with mascara. There are less ways to screw it up."

After dropping Nina off, I went home to find my mom watching movies on the Hallmark Channel and eating her way through a bag of Double Stuf Oreos.

"Tough day at the office?" I asked.

She patted a spot on the couch beside her. "I know that I became a relationship counselor to help people, but listening to someone else's issues all day can be a bummer."

I sat and grabbed an Oreo. "I'm guessing the guidance counselors didn't share that with you when you were picking
a major."

"No." She tilted her head and looked at my face. "I like the new makeup. Any special reason?"

"Just expressing my individualism."

"As long as you're doing it for yourself." She grabbed another Oreo and twisted the top off. "Or is there a guy in the picture?"

"There might be a new guy at school who is cute and artsy and maybe I'm trying to break out of my nerdy cocoon to become a slightly less nerdy butterfly."

"You are already a beautiful, short, nerdy butterfly, just like your short nerdy mom and grandmother."

No woman in our family made it past the five-foot-two mark. We were a short, bookish tribe. "Do we have plans for dinner?"

She pointed at the package of Oreos and feigned confusion. "This isn't dinner?"

While my mom gave great relationship advice to other people, she sucked at nutrition. "That's dessert."

"It's all a matter of opinion," she said.

I went into the kitchen and opened the freezer. Did I want something fast or something good? It felt like a vegetable lasagna night. I set the lasagna on the counter and preheated the oven. Then I joined my mom in the living room and grabbed a red scarf I'd been working on from my yarn basket beside the couch.

"I love that color," my mom said.

"Me, too." I held the scarf up and checked to make sure the rows were even. "I might keep this one."

Chapter Four

Matt

When I went to meet Lisa at her locker, the same way I did every morning, I did a double-take. Instead of her normal clothes, she wore some sort of green shirt and tight jeans tucked into her boots. The fact that she was a girl was way more obvious. And her lips sparkled and her eyes stood out, and wait a minute…she was looking right at me.

"Earth to Matt," she said. "How do you like the new me?"

What the hell do I say to that? My knee-jerk response was to tell her she didn't look like herself, but I had a sister and I knew that answer would land me on Lisa's shit list. "You look good. A little much for school, but good."

"Thanks," she said. "I think."

I wasn't the only guy noticing that my short, book loving friend suddenly seemed datable. Guys were checking her out. Soon she wouldn't be available to hang out with, because someone was going to ask her on a date. *Why does that thought annoy me?*

"Did someone not have enough Cap'n Crunch this morning?" Lisa asked.

"No. I had my normal two bowls."

"Then why are you out of it?"

I wanted to tell her she'd thrown what I thought of her out of whack. But before I'd friend-zoned her, she'd had a crush on me, and I wouldn't want to make it sound like I was interested in her, because I wasn't.

"It's Tuesday. We're at school. You're dressed like a pirate. Take your pick."

"Do you see any ruffles on this shirt?" she asked.

"Is that a trick question?" 'Cause there were definitely some curves there but I didn't think that was what she was talking about.

"Everyone knows pirates wear ruffled shirts. This shirt has no ruffles. Therefore I couldn't possibly be a pirate."

Who did Lisa remind me of? Jane. That was weird. Her pirate comment was just the type of thing Jane would say.

The bell rang so we headed for homeroom. Mine was next to hers so we walked together. And damn it if Trey didn't come walking toward us. He spotted Lisa and said, "Hey, soul mate."

She laughed and kept on walking.

Lisa ducked into her homeroom before I could ask what the hell that had been about.

Lisa and I didn't have any classes together since she was Miss Overachiever and I didn't see the point in working that hard. What had Trey meant with that soul mate line? Lisa had laughed. Must be an inside joke. When had they become so damn chummy?

By lunch I was on a slow burn. When I went to sit down at our normal table with her, Nina, and West, the happy expression Lisa had worn this morning was gone.

"What's wrong?" I asked.

"Nothing." She frowned and pulled a piece of string cheese apart, but didn't bother eating it.

"Uh-huh." I opened my lunch and took a bite of my ham sandwich. Might as well eat while I waited for her to start talking. Eventually, she'd share. Another thing I'd learned from my sister: girls weren't the type to suffer in silence.

"Can you explain guy logic to me?" she asked.

"Maybe." I wiped my mouth with a napkin. "Depends on the guy."

"You heard Trey this morning. I thought he was flirting with me."

"What was that comment about?"

"He heard me gripe about how much I hated Mondays. He joked we might be soul mates. We talked on the way into school."

Now I got it. "He probably was flirting with you this morning, but he might be the kind of guy who flirts with every pretty girl he meets."

Lisa tilted her head and looked at me funny. "You think I'm pretty?"

Son of a...why did I say that? "You're cute. You know that." I took a drink of my soda like it was no big deal.

"Okay...back to the topic at hand. This morning he went out of his way to talk to me. I've seen him twice since then and I didn't even get that weird head nod of recognition you guys do. What does that mean?"

How honest should I be? "Not trying to be a jerk, but the guy just moved here. He has options. He's probably not looking for a steady girlfriend."

"Is any guy ever looking for a girlfriend?" Lisa asked. "Because most of the time, guys seem to resist the idea of dating one person."

"Maybe they resist it until they find the right person," Nina said from my other side. "And once they find that person life is full of unicorns and rainbows. Right, West?"

"Yes." West nodded in an exaggerated way, clearly not meaning what he said. "That's exactly how it works."

I laughed. Lisa didn't. One of the things I liked about Lisa was she didn't fly off the handle like most girls I knew.

"Listen. This Trey guy might like you. He might like everyone. Why focus on him?"

She took a Twinkie out of her bag and broke it in half before taking a bite. "I don't know. I liked the idea of starting fresh with someone. I can be whoever I want to be."

"You can do that without him," I said.

"How?" She gestured around the cafeteria. "I've been going to school with everyone here for years. They all have this idea of who I am."

"That annoying girl in class who knows all the answers?" I teased.

She poked me in the ribs. "I am not annoying."

"Fine." I grinned. "You're not that annoying. You're just a nerd-girl who knows almost all of the answers."

"Better than a guy who skates by making C's when he's smart enough to do better."

"I told you. I have a system. Make A's for the first half of the semester and then stop studying so I can glide down into the C range."

"That is not a plan," Lisa said. "It's self-sabotage."

I pointed at her. "Not a therapist."

She pointed back at me. "Maybe I'll become a therapist just like my mom to spite you. I'll track you down after college and tell you all the things you're compensating for."

I snorted.

"Allow me to tell you your future," Lisa continued. "You'll graduate from high school and continue working with your dad in your family landscaping business. He'll badger you into taking some business classes to help you learn how to run the company. You'll be at your happiest when you're outside planting things in the sunshine."

"Sounds about right," I said. "Now I'm going to tell you your future. You'll get some sort of degree and become a writer or a librarian. One day you'll call me and ask me to landscape your house with books."

She laughed. "I'd never disrespect books like that. Although I did see this thing on Pinterest where they painted bricks to look like the spines of books and decorated someone's garden with them."

"That could be kind of cool," I said, and then I grinned. "Wait...that's probably the opposite of cool."

"Nerd-girls rule." Lisa sat up straighter. "And we'll probably end up ruling the world."

"You probably will. It's a good thing we're on friendly terms."

After school I headed out to the parking lot with West and Nina.

"Can I talk to you for a minute?" Nina asked.

"Sure." I followed her to West's car. "What's up?"

"Don't mess with Lisa's head."

What was she talking about? "You lost me."

"Seriously," Nina said. "Pick a lane."

"I have no idea what you're talking about."

"You told her she was pretty. You don't tell a girl that unless you like her."

I backed away from her. "You're way off base."

"Or you're delusional," Nina shot back as I headed off to my ride.

Yeah. Right. Like I wanted to date Lisa.

Chapter Five

Lisa

After dinner, I helped my mom with the dishes while I mulled over what Matt had said.

"What has you so quiet?" my mom asked.

"Just trying to figure out how guys think."

She laughed and handed me the salad bowl to dry. "Not an easy problem to solve. What's going on?"

I told her about Trey, and Matt's spin on the situation. "Any professional words of wisdom?"

She handed me a plate. "I'd say live your life the way you want and eventually you'll find someone who makes you happy."

"That is not solid advice." I dried the plate and put it away in the cabinet above the coffeemaker.

"Let's look at the big picture. You don't know much about Trey besides the fact that he's cute, has cool hair, and occasionally he's funny." She passed me another plate. "Matt seems like a solid guy. No matter who you date, you should still live your life with your goals."

"Speaking of living your life and having goals, what's the end goal for you and Tony?"

She handed me the salad tongs. "For now, we're happy with the way things are. We've talked about moving in together after you graduate."

"You know you don't have to wait for me to graduate." I liked Tony. He made my mom happy and he didn't treat me like a little kid. He talked to me like a rational human being.

"Tony and I both have our reasons for waiting. We're happy with the status quo."

As I put the salad tongs away, I tried to figure out how to ask my next question. There was no subtle way to do it, so I jumped in with both feet. "Do you still believe in marriage?"

She paused with her hands in the soapy water. "That's a hard question to answer. I believe in it for other people and

I want you to believe in it."

I leaned my hip against the counter. "After knowing what the sperm donor did, the idea of marriage seems like building a house on quicksand."

"There are a lot of successful relationships and happy marriages out there. Don't let what happened to me keep you from following your heart."

"Right now I can't even find a guy to date," I said. "So you don't have to worry about lifelong relationships."

My mom's cell rang. She checked it, frowned, and then let it go to voicemail.

I didn't recognize the number on the screen. "Who was that?"

"Some guy who keeps booking appointments and then canceling them. After the third time, I stopped taking his calls because he refused to pay the cancellation fee, and he felt the need to tell me how busy he was and how I needed to be more flexible. Someone will make a mint off that narcissistic jackass and they are welcome to it."

I laughed.

"That was an unprofessional mom rant, so please don't repeat it to anyone."

"No worries," I said.

There seemed to be two kinds of people that went to counselors: those who needed help recovering or getting through a rough patch and those who wanted the therapist to stroke their egos and tell them they were in the right and everyone else was wrong.

I put away the last dish and my cell rang. It was Matt. My heart skipped a beat. *Stop it. We're just friends.* That had become my mantra. "Hey, Matt. What's up?"

"I got roped into hanging out at Bixby's with Charlie while he waits for Clarissa's shift to end. Some kid is having her eighth birthday party and she's dressed like Hermione."

"That's so cute."

"Yeah, it's a thrill a minute. Want to come meet us and save me from dying of boredom? I'll throw in some cheese fries to make it worth the trip."

I'd finished my homework before dinner. "Sure. I'll be there in fifteen minutes."

When I hung up, my mom was smiling at me like she knew something I didn't. "What?"

"That boy likes you. He just hasn't admitted it to himself."

He'd made it clear that he wasn't interested. "Nope. He's just bored."

I brushed my teeth and checked my reflection in the mirror. My hair was working its way free from the braid I'd put in this morning so I twisted it up into a bun. Half my eyeliner was gone, so I washed my face and reapplied my normal pink gloss. It was Matt, so I didn't need to go all out. When I pulled up to the restaurant, a retro fifties diner, I could see little kids whacking a Voldemort piñata with a broom. Someone had a cool mom.

I found Matt and Charlie sitting at a booth as far away from the kid party as possible. "Afraid you'll get smacked with the broom?" I asked as I slid onto the bench next to Matt.

"They already took out half a dozen drinks." Matt pointed at an area that must have been recently mopped. It sported those yellow safety signs warning people to be careful of the wet floors.

Clarissa came over to our table. Charlie's eyes lit up as she came closer. He must really be into her. What would it be like to have someone look at me like that...like they couldn't wait to be near me?

"Cheese fries and a soda?" Clarissa said to me.

That was my normal order. "After seeing their ice- cream cake, I want a brownie sundae instead."

"My personal favorite," Clarissa said. "Be back in a minute."

After my sundae arrived, Matt said, "I've never understood ice cream with cake. It makes the cake soggy."

"Not if you eat it fast enough." I demonstrated by shoving a giant spoonful of ice cream-covered brownie into my mouth.

He passed me a napkin. "Try smaller bites."

I wiped my face and the napkin came away with whipped cream and chocolate sauce. "Oops."

"I can't take you anywhere," he teased.

Matt was smiling and his eyes were bright and he was close enough that I could feel the heat coming off his body. And a tiny voice in the back of my brain wondered why this couldn't be real. He obviously liked spending time with me. If he wasn't hung up on Jane, would something have happened between us? No sense going down that road because Jane was around and Matt was hooked on her and that was that. Besides, I didn't want to be anyone's second choice or consolation prize.

One of the kids whacked the Voldemort piñata so hard it busted open and Tootsie Rolls in every flavor rained down. "That's not Harry Potter candy," I said. "It doesn't go

with the theme."

The kids scampered around grabbing the brightly colored candy from the floor.

"They don't seem to mind," Matt said.

"If you're going to pick a theme," I said, "you should commit."

"Okay, nerd-girl. If you'd planned the party, what would you have put in the piñata?"

I set my spoon down. "I'm not sure you're ready for this conversation, but here we go. There are Bertie Bott's Every Flavor Beans. There are chocolate frogs, and fizzing whizbees, and—"

"Stop." Matt held his hands up in surrender. "I never should have questioned your Harry Potter knowledge."

"I am the queen of nerd-girl knowledge," I said in a fake haughty voice.

"That you are." Matt grinned and my heart raced and I really needed it to stop doing that when I was around him because my brain knew better.

Chapter Six

Matt

Lisa seemed so much happier now than she had been at school. I liked seeing her happy. If that Trey guy was who she wanted, then maybe I could help her. I had an idea that might solve both of our problems. It was a little out there. Would she go for it? Only one way to find out.

I leaned in and spoke in a quiet voice so no one could overhear. "I wanted to talk to you about this whole dating thing."

She stopped chewing for a moment and stared at me.

Then she swallowed and wiped off her mouth. "Go on."

"You want Trey. You know who I'm into. I've seen how girls flirt with West more since he has a girlfriend. You and I could pretend to date. I mean we hang out together all the time anyway. Maybe the people we're interested in would take notice."

She sat back and squinted at me like I was insane. "You want to fake-date me? I find that mildly insulting."

"What? No. It's not."

"How do you figure?" She sounded ticked off.

"You're the one who talked about the wedding ring effect and people wanting what they can't have."

"When you put it that way, I'm not nearly as annoyed." She ate a few more bites of brownie. "That could work. People always seem to want what they can't have."

"Right."

"If we did this, and that's a giant *if*, how would it work?"

Good question. I hadn't thought that far ahead. "I don't know, oh Queen of nerd-dom. You're the smart one. Use
your big brain. What do you think we should do?"

She took another bite of her sundae and seemed to consider it. "When you think about it, we pretty much look like a couple already. If you put your arm around my shoulders or if we hold hands in public, that would clue people in."

"Sounds good." We'd need some ground rules, because I wouldn't want this to backfire...for her to think this could really turn into something between us because that option was not on the table. "If neither of the people we want notice and nothing happens, we'll stage a friendly breakup in a few weeks."

"What about Nina?" she asked. "I don't want to lie to her."

"You also don't want her accidentally blabbing about what we're doing because then there's no way it will work."

She stirred the ice cream around in her bowl. "I'm going to have to think about this."

"Whatever." I sat back and took a drink of my soda. It's not like I actually wanted to date Lisa. Was she hesitating because she used to be into me? Maybe I'd read that situation wrong. Maybe she'd never wanted to be more than friends.

When it came to reading girls, I didn't have a great track record. As soon as things became complicated, I bailed. Not to be a dick but I always thought when I found the right person the pieces would fall into place. When I finally found the right girl, being around her should be easy and comfortable. Relationships shouldn't have to be so much work. My dad and my mom just clicked together. While my mom could be a little out-there sometimes, my dad always calmed her down. He was the calm to her storm. And now it's like I was thinking song lyrics. *What the hell is wrong with me?*

Lisa shoved her half-eaten brownie sundae away and wiped her hands on a napkin. "I should go."

And now things were weird. Damn it. I didn't want to ruin our friendship. I reached for her hand. "I'm sorry. It was a stupid idea."

"I don't know," she said. "I never thought us dating was a terrible idea."

Wait. Did she mean real or fake dating?

Her cheeks turned red. She cleared her throat. "I mean fake dating could work for a while. And if nothing comes of it after a few weeks we re-evaluate the situation."

"Sounds good to me."

"Oh my gosh." Clarissa came toward us, pointing at our intertwined hands. "Did Matt finally figure it out and ask you on a date?"

Lisa froze for a second, like a deer in headlights. Like she wasn't sure which way to run. She turned to me and raised her eyebrows. Like she would go along with whatever I said, so I dove in.

"Yes. I finally did. But she hasn't answered me yet."

Lisa tilted her head and studied me. "Are you sure you want to leave the friend zone?"

I nodded.

"Okay," she said. "We'll give it a try."

"Oh, that's so exciting." Clarissa slid into the bench seat next to Charlie. He was giving me the you're-an-idiot look. Had he overheard our conversation? Probably. I never thought of keeping anything from him. I knew he'd never rat me out. Maybe it was a twin thing.

"We still have a few things to figure out," Lisa told her. "But I think this might work."

Clarissa smiled. "I don't know what took him so long.

Anyone can see you two belong together."

I snorted. "I wouldn't go that far."

Lisa glared at me. "Do you want this to be the shortest relationship in history?"

"Just joking," I said, even though I kind of wasn't.

"He's always been a little slow," Charlie said.

"I could point out that you needed Nina to get Clarissa's phone number." I toasted him with my drink.

"Doesn't matter." Clarissa leaned into Charlie and he put his arm around her shoulders. "It's kind of cute that he was too shy to ask me himself."

I snorted. "Yeah, he's freaking adorable."

"I am," Charlie said. "Apparently I'm the twin with the looks *and* the brains."

Lisa chuckled. "What does that leave Matt?"

"He's better at coming up with dumb-ass schemes," Charlie said. "So there's that."

I flipped him off.

"Enough male bonding," Clarissa said. "I'm off work and I want to get out of here."

Charlie and Clarissa slid out of their side of the booth.

We followed along, heading out to the parking lot.

Chapter Seven

Lisa

Had I lost my freaking mind? That was the question that played on repeat in my head as we followed Clarissa and Charlie out into the cool evening air. What had I just agreed to? Why had I gone along with this? Maybe I'd been lulled into a false sense of serenity from the sugar and chocolate in the brownie sundae. That, combined with my body being too close to Matt's, had messed up my brain waves.

I wasn't sure which bothered me more: the fact that Matt only thought I was good enough to pretend-date or the fact that I considered keeping the truth from Nina.

We said our goodbyes to Clarissa and Charlie and then Matt followed me over to my car. With every step across the parking lot, doubt bounced around in my brain. The pessimistic part of my personality wanted to tell him to forget this whole crazy scheme because no one would give a crap we were dating. My positive side pointed out that Clarissa had noticed, so other people might pay some attention, too. It was interesting that I wasn't the only person who thought Matt and I would make a good couple. Anyone who'd been wondering why we weren't dating would take note of our new situation. That could propel me into the datable range for people who might never have paid attention to me before. So even if Trey wasn't influenced by this strange dating experiment, other guys might see me as someone they'd want to ask out.

Was this idea insane or genius? I didn't know. At least it was better than the non-datable friend zone area I'd been living in lately. Still, I needed to talk to someone about the strange detour my dating life had taken to get some perspective on how bat-shit crazy this idea really was. And there was only one person I'd risk confessing the truth to. When we reached my car, I said, "I'm not going to lie to Nina."

"Your choice." He stood there awkwardly with his hands shoved in his front jeans pockets.

He didn't have to look so enthusiastic about the situation. This was his stupid idea. I felt like giving him some grief or throwing him off balance so I said, "If we were really dating, you'd kiss me goodbye." How would he react to that statement?

He came closer and reached out to run his fingers down my cheek in a light caress that made my skin tingle and my heart beat faster. His eyes locked onto mine and his gaze drifted down to my lips and then back up to my eyes. "No, I wouldn't," he said, "because if I really liked a girl I wouldn't want our first kiss to be in some crappy parking lot." He dropped his hand and stepped back from me. "See you tomorrow at your locker."

As Matt walked away, my heart fought to return to its normal rhythm. That hadn't worked out how I expected it. He was supposed to be thrown off kilter, not me.

I climbed into my car and drove home in record time. Once I was in my room, I dialed Nina and told her everything, ending the gush of information with, "So what do you think?"

A slightly judgmental silence came through the phone for a moment before Nina said, "You still like him, don't you?"

My brain replayed the sensation of his fingers caressing my cheek. "No. I don't know. Maybe."

"Have you thought this through?" Nina asked. "Because there are so many ways this could go bad."

"You think I don't know that?" I practically yelled into the phone. "Best case scenario, Trey sees me as datable and asks me out after Matt and I break up. Worst case scenario, Trey doesn't give a rat's ass I'm dating someone. Matt and I break up, and then I have to spend the rest of my senior year pretending to be okay with just being Matt's friend."

"Maybe there's another way this could go," Nina said. "Matt could realize you two *are* meant to be together. And we could have a lot of fun trying to push him in that direction."

My brain felt fried from running through all the terrible ways this could explode in my face. "What do you mean?"

"There's nothing to say you can't continue trying new looks...maybe sexier looks...looks that will make him regret that what's going on between you isn't real."

I laughed. "Maybe if I was some sexy femme fatale, but I'm not."

"You could be," Nina said. "He's the one suggesting you act like a couple. I say play it up for all it's worth. Who knows, maybe both Matt and Trey will be into you and you'll get to choose who you want for your boyfriend."

"Yeah, right. In case you can't tell, I'm doing a major eye roll."

"If you don't want to try and reel him in, then you need to squash your crush."

"I thought I had." I moaned and lay back on the bed. "Then he touched my face and smiled at me and my crush reared back to life."

"On the plus side, we can officially double-date now," Nina said.

"By all means, ignore my emotional upheaval and figure out how this benefits your agenda." I was only partially joking.

"Hey, I'm trying to look on the bright side. Think of it as a social experiment."

I stared up at my ceiling. "Maybe I could write a paper on it. The Theory of How Guys Are Idiots and Only Want What They Can't Have."

"Whatever you do, don't let Matt know you told me the truth."

"Why not?"

"Because if I think the relationship is real, then he'll have to act out the part."

"Huh." That wasn't a bad idea. Then again, I wasn't a good liar. "Life is complicated enough. I'm going to stick to the truth."

"Well, I'm still going to give him crap."

"I never doubted that for a second." I laughed. Nina's favorite form of entertainment was arguing. When I wasn't the one she was arguing with, it was kind of amusing to watch.

"There's one thing you have to remember," Nina said. "What's that?"

"If it starts to feel real for you but it's fake for him, you need to break it off."

"How will I know if he has any real feelings for me? It's not like he's the chatty type."

"No, but from what I've seen, he's honest."

"Pointing out that he's a good guy doesn't help the situation because it only emphasizes the fact that someone who is boyfriend material doesn't see me as girlfriend material."

"It's not too late to back out," Nina said. "It's not like you signed some contract."

"I know, but if I don't try this then nothing changes. What's that saying? The definition of insanity is doing the same thing over and over again and expecting different results. If I want my life to change for the better, I think I need to switch it up a little bit."

"Okay then, Operation Fake Boyfriend is on."

Chapter Eight

Matt

I'd lost my freaking mind. That was the only explanation. Fake dating a girl who was one of my best friends was a terrible idea. If Clarissa hadn't forced the issue, Lisa would have shut me down. It was the stupidest idea in dating history. No way she wouldn't end up pissed off at me. And then I'd lose her as a friend. She was the one girl I could be comfortable around who didn't want anything from me, and I was about to screw it all up, hoping that Jane might notice me. Then there was the minor detail of Jane's perfect boyfriend. He'd have to be out of the picture. Short of running him down with my car and burying him with the backhoe, I didn't see Jane's relationship ending anytime soon.

Maybe I should call this whole stupid thing off. I poured myself a second bowl of Cap'n Crunch and grabbed the milk from the refrigerator. Charlie came into the kitchen and made a bowl of Lucky Charms. It was one of the few things we don't agree on. I don't know how he can eat that crap. Marshmallows in cereal are gross.

"Sure you don't want some?" He shook the box at me. "After that dumb-ass move you pulled yesterday, you can use all the luck you can get."

I flipped him off while I chewed and swallowed. "Your girlfriend is the one who forced the issue."

"And your girlfriend could have told her the truth."

"She's not my girlfriend," I said.

"Keep telling yourself that," Charlie shot back.

This was no big deal. That's what I told myself as I walked toward Lisa's locker. She'd spotted me, crossed her arms over her chest, and smiled like she knew a secret.

I couldn't help but smile back. Maybe this wouldn't be so bad.

When I reached her, she said, "Good morning. Did you have nightmares about little kids swinging at you with brooms like you were a Voldemort piñata?"

"No." I scratched my head, trying to remember what I'd dreamed. "It was something about taking a test I hadn't studied for."

"Isn't that your normal life?"

"Pretty much." I grinned. She got me. I liked that. One of the reasons I liked being around Lisa was because I didn't have to put on some cool guy act. I could be myself. While she might give me crap, she didn't try to tell me what to do, like some girls I'd dated in the past.

Nina joined us with West in tow. "It's so exciting. Now that you guys are together we can double-date."

I checked with West. "What's she talking about?"

"She drank a double espresso on the way to school," West said. "It's best to smile and nod until the caffeine wears off."

"Come on," Nina enthused. "It will be fun. We can go to the movies together and out to eat. Or, I know...we could go bowling."

Hadn't Lisa told Nina the truth about our fake relationship? Odds were she had, and Nina was just giving me grief. "Yeah...I didn't sign up for that."

"Relax," Lisa said, "she's not suggesting we hold hands and sing Kumbaya."

"Although that could be fun," Nina said. "Oh, wait. I know. We could do karaoke."

"I call a veto on that last idea," Lisa said.

"Good call." I had no desire to stand in front of people and fake sing a song.

Nina laughed. "Fine. We'll do something normal, like go to the movies or out to eat."

"You realize we do most of those things together already," Lisa said.

"Yes, but now that you're officially dating." She glanced at me. "It will be a lot more fun."

"So we weren't fun before?" Lisa said and then she looked at me. "I might be offended."

Nina turned to her boyfriend. "Explain it to them."

West pointed at her. "This is my girlfriend, Nina. She's slightly crazy. I have to live with her so it would be best to go along with her plans and pretend to be excited."

Lisa laughed. I did too because that was the only way to make it through this strange conversation. The bell rang, signaling it was time to head to homeroom. Lisa and I walked together like we did every day.

"It's funny," Lisa said. "But we already do a lot of things that couples do."

"You mean like hanging out with Nina and West?"

"No. Like walking to homeroom and eating lunch together."

She was right. "I never thought of it like that."

"That's probably why Clarissa thought we should date."

"Probably."

"Here's a question. What happens when we break up? Do we still meet at my locker and talk in the morning?"

I hadn't thought that far ahead. "Maybe not at first."

"I guess we'll figure it out as we go along. See you later." Lisa turned into her homeroom and I kept walking.

Leaving things to chance didn't seem like a great idea, especially when Nina seemed determined to give me grief. Normally, I was all about going with the flow, but maybe we could set some ground rules. I'd ask Lisa about it at lunch.

...

At lunch, once we were seated, I said, "Are you busy after school?"

She shook her head no, since she'd just taken a bite of her turkey sandwich. After swallowing, she said, "Why?"

"I thought we could hang out and talk—figure out how this dating thing is going to work."

She grinned. "You don't like improvising, do you?"

"No."

"I'm not sure you can plan these things, but sure. I don't work tonight, so we can get together."

• • •

After school, I followed Lisa back to her house. I'd never been to her place before. It was in an older section of town... still nice, but man, the houses were small. Not like my house was huge, but it was comfortable. Lisa's house looked like something a kid had built out of brick-colored Legos.

I parked my truck in front of her house. The good thing about this end of town was streets were wide and parking was easy. Somehow, the wide expanse of pavement made the houses look smaller. Maybe it was an optical illusion. I followed Lisa in through the front door where I walked across the living room in five strides. Not an illusion. This place was tiny. Two small recliners I'd be afraid to sit in and a small couch filled up the entire space. "This place is like a doll house."

"We're small people, so we don't need a lot of space," Lisa said in a way that could have been defensive, but it wasn't. She was stating a fact and wasn't really bothered by the size of the house.

We headed into the kitchen. I hoped it would be bigger. Nope. If I stretched my arms out I could almost touch both walls. I was starting to feel claustrophobic. Sliding glass doors showed blue lawn chairs and an umbrella table set up on the back patio and that was where I wanted to go.

"Can we sit outside?" I'd been cooped up inside all day at school and I wanted to breathe some fresh air.

"Sure." She flipped the latch and slid the glass doors open. I stepped outside, taking in a lungful of air that smelled like wood smoke and grass. There was nothing but grass in the front and backyard which seemed kind of sad. "You guys need some landscaping."

"You might like playing in the dirt, but my mom doesn't and neither do I. We pay the guy next door to mow the grass. It works for us."

She sat in one of the blue chairs, and I did the same. "What did you want to talk about?" she asked.

Why did it feel like I was on a job interview? "Well...we kind of jumped into this," I said. "We might need a game plan."

"Is that what we're doing?" She tilted her head and studied me. "Playing a dating game?"

I nodded. "Pretty much, and when this is over, I still want to be friends."

"Me, too. So do we put a time limit on it? Like if Trey doesn't make a move, we give up after a month and tell everyone we worked better as friends?"

"Sounds good."

"You realize we'll have to double-date with Nina and West," she said.

"I know you told her the truth."

"I did," Lisa said. "But she's been dying for me to find a boyfriend so we could double-date. You've met her, so you know there's no point arguing."

"I used to think West was stubborn, but she's worse."

"Maybe that's why they work so well together," Lisa said.

"I don't know. Dating your neighbor seems like a bad idea. When they break up, it's going to be awkward."

Lisa leaned toward me. Her forehead was scrunched up like she was confused or maybe angry. "What do you mean, *when* they break up? Why do you think they're going to break up?"

Angry...definitely angry. "Everyone breaks up."

"That's a shitty attitude."

"I'm being realistic." Why was she getting mad about this?

"Good thing this is a fake relationship because if it wasn't, that would be a huge red flag that you can't be serious about a girl."

"That's not true." I stood. "Since this isn't real, there's no need for us to fight about it. I'll see you at school tomorrow."

"Seriously?" Lisa said. "You're going to bail in the middle of a conversation?"

"It's a stupid conversation."

"Wow. We veer away from the friend zone for twenty-four hours and you turn into a dick. Good to know." She stood and headed into the house, slamming the patio door.

Well, hell. Did I go after her to smooth this over or leave? Leaving would be the easiest thing to do, but I didn't want to lose her as a friend so I headed back into the house.

She was sitting on the couch in the living room eating from a bag of Oreos.

What could I say? Best to stick with the truth. "I have no idea what just happened."

"I can sum it up in two words. Commitment phobic. The idea of being in a relationship with one girl makes you panic. I don't get it. I've seen you in dating action. It's not like you're a player. You pay attention to a girl for a while, and then as soon as she starts coming around on a regular basis, you lose interest. We should call this whole fake dating thing off, because friend-you I like. Boyfriend-you I don't."

I ran my hand back through my hair. I needed a few weeks to see if Jane would notice me. Not that she'd dump Mr. Perfect, but if they ever broke up she might see me as boyfriend material. "Give me three weeks. After that, you can sign on for longer if Trey hasn't noticed you, or you can dump me."

She pried open an Oreo and ate the side with the icing. "Promise not to be a dick?" she said.

"I'll do my best."

"Okay, then I'll give you three weeks."

Chapter Nine

Lisa

After Matt left, I finished off two more Oreos. Was this a mistake? How could friend-Matt be so nice while Boyfriend-Matt was such a tool? Maybe it was a good thing we weren't really dating. I didn't get it. Why would he think all relationships were destined to end? He was one of the few people I knew whose parents were still together. You'd think he'd have a more positive outlook on life.

It was going to be a strange three weeks. There was no way I was going to agree to a longer pretend relationship if this was how Matt was going to act. It's not like I believed in happily ever after, but knowing he thought a breakup was unavoidable made him a lot less appealing. Maybe that was a good thing. This experience would definitely end my crush. Still...finding out he wasn't boyfriend material was kind of like finding out the Easter Bunny wasn't real.

That was okay. I'd focus on Trey. He was the whole reason I'd agreed to this fake dating debacle in the first place.

•••

For the next few days Matt and I were civil to each other at school. It felt weird, fake, and wrong.

"What's going on between you and Matt?" Clarissa asked in gym class as she, Nina, and I walked around the track.

I inhaled a lungful of cool air and blew it out, stalling for time. "Why do you ask?"

"Since you two started dating you seem less happy.

That's not how it's supposed to work," she said.

Whatever I told her might get back to Trey so I needed to stick to something close to the truth. "I don't know. Dating is harder than being friends. Sometimes I think we never should have left the friend zone."

41

"I'm sorry," Clarissa said. "Do you want me to ask Charlie to talk to him?"

God, no. I shook my head. "That would make it more awkward. Maybe we're going through some sort of adjustment period."

"Again," she said, "that's not how it's supposed to work."

"Topic change," I declared. "What's up with your cousin Trey?"

"His parents moved from Chicago because his dad lost his job."

"That kind of sucks."

"They only moved there because of his job," Clarissa said. "I think they're happy to be back. Trey wasn't thrilled to switch schools, but he's pretty cool. He paints and draws. He already has groupies in art class."

I laughed, even though the idea of him having groupies gave me a small moment of panic. "It's his hair," I joked. "Isn't it?"

"Probably," she agreed. "He may not hate the move as much as he claims, because his girlfriend dumped him for a college guy."

That bit of information gave me hope. Not that I was happy he'd been dumped, but if he'd had a girlfriend, then he might be boyfriend material, and it also proved he wasn't afraid of relationships. Good to know. Especially since Matt didn't seem too hip on the idea.

My fake boyfriend stood near my locker after school, looking at his cell. I took a moment to appreciate the way he filled out his blue flannel shirt and his jeans. Some guys might look like hicks. He just looked...huggable. When he glanced up and smiled at me my heart did a little tap dance...and that was wrong. *It's fake. Fake. Fake. Fake.*

"Hey." He lowered his phone. "West asked if we wanted to go to the movies with him and Nina tomorrow."

That could be a low pressure situation because we wouldn't have to deal with the awkward conversations we seemed to be having lately. "What movie?"

He laughed. "Shouldn't you say yes to the date first and then ask about the movie?"

"I must have missed that lesson in how-to-date-like-a-normal-girl class."

"Not sure you fall under the category of normal," he shot back. "There're a couple of action movies."

He passed me his phone with the theater information pulled up. I scanned past a violent horror flick that no mentally healthy person should want to see, and skipped over one of those movies where they try to make everyone cry by killing off the main character's love interest. I never understood the point of those movies. That whole cathartic crying thing was crap. There was a movie about computers taking over the planet. Those were usually entertaining, as long as the people weren't too stupid. There was a bank robbery movie and something about vampires and humans teaming up against zombies.

"I'm in for the evil computers or the vampire movie." I preferred things that couldn't possibly happen in real life.

"Either one works for me," he said.

"Good." *Now what?*

He shoved his phone in his pocket and glanced around like someone might be watching us. "Want to walk out to the parking lot together?"

"Sure. That seems like a couple-y thing to do."

"Couple-y?"

"Something couples do."

"Yeah." He scratched his head. "I'm pretty sure that's not a word."

"It is now."

"You should create your own online dictionary."

"Not a bad idea. I can call it Lisa's Lexicon."

"Lexi what?"

"Lexicon. I didn't make that one up. It means vocabulary."

"And you couldn't just say that?"

"Nope." I grinned. "The double *L* sounds better."

"Sure it does." He gestured down the hall. "Let's get out of here."

We joined the crowd of students shuffling past each other, eager to get out of the building. Most of the couples were holding hands. Wondering how Matt would react, I reached for his hand. He missed a step and looked down at our joined hands.

"Now who's confused about the rules of dating?" I pointed at the couple in front of us.

"A little warning would be nice."

He sounded annoyed and that kind of ticked me off. "So sorry I got girl germs on you." I pulled my hand from his like I was joking, even though I wasn't.

He laughed. "I stopped being afraid of girl germs a long time ago." He grabbed my hand and laced his fingers through mine. "I don't like surprises."

We exited the building and headed for the parking lot. "You must be really fun at surprise birthday parties."

"The good thing about being a twin is you're not the only person standing there feeling stupid while people sing to you."

"Why would having someone sing happy birthday make you feel stupid?"

"I don't like being the center of attention."

Something clicked into place. "Charlie talks more than you."

Matt nodded.

"You're the quieter twin." I'd never thought of it that way. It explained a few things, like maybe why he'd never asked Jane on a date.

The gravel of the parking lot crunched under our feet as we angled left toward my car. Once we came to a stop, I noticed the other real couples were kissing each other goodbye. I felt like giving Matt a little crap. "Fair warning since you are surprise-phobic. At some point you might have to kiss me, just to convince people this is real."

He dropped my hand and backed away from me like I hadn't bathed in a week. "Not going to happen."

"Wow." That kind of stung. "You really know how to make a girl feel special." I climbed into my car, slammed the door, and locked it. What was his problem? I'd been joking. Still, I hadn't expected him to recoil in disgust.

Matt knocked on the window. "Lisa?"

Nope. I flipped him off, put the car in reverse, and backed out of my parking spot. Dating Matt was supposed to make Trey see me as datable. Having Matt act all awkward around me was not upping my cool points. It made me seem *less* datable. And I wasn't okay with that. So far Operation Fake Boyfriend was a complete waste of time.

As soon as I entered my house, I called Nina and unloaded on her.

"That's so weird," Nina said. "I mean, maybe he doesn't want to be your real boyfriend, but why would he freak out about the idea of kissing you?"

"I don't know. Maybe he thinks I'll fall madly in love with him." The odds of that happening weren't good, especially since he was being such a jerk.

"It's weird that he could be a good friend and make such a terrible fake boyfriend," Nina said. "Unless maybe he's afraid he'll fall for you."

"Right." I laughed. "He wants a quirky blonde, not a boringly normal brunette."

"You're not boring."

"You have to say that because you're my friend." I lay back on my bed and closed my eyes. "Is it wrong that I want to find some way to torment him?"

"No. I'd say that's healthy. And I think the movie date will be the perfect way to do that."

"Game on."

Chapter Ten

Matt

Okay. I'd messed up. Now Lisa was mad. I didn't mean to make it sound like kissing her would be terrible. She was cute in her own nerdy bookworm kind of way. It's just that I never thought of her like that. And kissing her could be awkward. What if it was terrible? It would be embarrassing for both of us. As far as I was concerned, it wasn't worth the risk.

When I'd come up with this brilliant fake dating plan I hadn't thought things through. I never imagined acting out the part of her boyfriend...never planned on kissing her. That was a bad idea. I wanted her as a friend. If I kissed her then it would be hard to go back to being friends. Especially if it *wasn't* terrible.

At this point she probably didn't want anything to do with me—friend or otherwise. How could I fix this? Maybe if I let her be, it would blow over by tomorrow.

•••

Friday morning it seemed like everyone was trying to figure out weekend plans. I already had plans for my double date with Lisa, but I wasn't sure if she still intended to go through with it. She hadn't said a word to me so far today. Why had I thought she'd let this go? I had a sister. I should have known better. At her locker this morning, she'd talked to Nina and stared at her phone and ignored my general existence.

Now lunch was almost over, and she'd spent the whole time avoiding eye contact with me while talking to our friends. Since Charlie ate lunch with Clarissa and her friends, that didn't leave me a lot of people to talk to. I checked the clock. We had ten minutes until the bell rang and then I wouldn't see her again until after school. The sub sandwich I'd eaten twisted around in my stomach. I needed to say something, but what?

I reached over and touched her arm. "Can we talk?"

She glanced at where my hand touched her arm and then met my gaze. "Careful. I might get the wrong idea. You wouldn't want me to think you actually liked me."

Okay. Still mad. I pulled my hand back. "I'm sorry about yesterday. I didn't mean that how it sounded."

She leaned closer. "Really? What did you mean?"

"I just...I don't know. I'm afraid kissing you might mess up our friendship and I didn't want things to get weird between us."

"Well that worked out *spectacularly*."

"I know. I'm sorry," I said. "Can you give me another chance?"

"To do what?" she said.

How did I answer that question? "To show you that I'm not the tool you think I am."

"This was your stupid idea so I don't understand why you're having such a problem with it. And I was joking about the kiss. You should have known that. Our friendship is based on joking around and giving each other crap. By the way, I liked friend-you but so far boyfriend-you sucks."

Not what I wanted Jane to see. "I'm aware. And maybe I freaked out because what I'm most afraid of is losing you as a friend."

She sighed. "If you'd said that instead of acting like I had the plague then maybe I wouldn't be so pissed off at you right now."

"Give me one more chance. I promise not to be a tool."

"I'm not sure you can help it," Lisa said. "It seems to be part of your DNA."

I knew she was insulting me on purpose to get back at me. "Feel better now?"

She held her fingers out like she was measuring something an inch long. "A little bit."

"Good, now can we go back to our plan?"

She stared at me for a moment like she was considering the deal. "I'll give you one more chance. One. Just remember, if we aren't friends once this is over, it's your fault."

"Got it. Are we still on for our double date?"

"I guess."

...

I pulled to a stop in front of Lisa's house later than night. For a second I considered honking the horn and hoping she'd run out, but that would be rude. I'd made enough of an ass of myself lately, so I parked and headed toward her front door, intent on doing the gentlemanly thing. She must have been watching for me because she came out the front door before I made it up the sidewalk.

"Hey." She came down the steps to meet me and something was very wrong. It looked like she'd forgotten to put on jeans. All I could see was her black coat and black boots that came up past her knees. Between the coat and the boots was some skintight black material. Definitely not pants. Definitely hot.

"Everything okay?" she asked in her normal friend voice which didn't match the non-friend thoughts invading my brain.

"Yeah," I said. "We should go."

Once we were in the truck, I kept my eyes on the road. Why had she worn whatever it was she was wearing? This was not a real date. It wasn't. She wasn't wearing that to look good for me. She must be wearing it so this would look like a date. Or maybe so Trey would see her and wish he'd asked her out. That thought made me tighten my hands on the steering wheel.

"Matt, did you hear me?"

Crap. "No. What did you say?"

"I asked you about popcorn. Buttered or plain?"

"Buttered."

"Good, then we can share because plain popcorn tastes like Styrofoam."

Okay, we were talking about popcorn. Time to focus on the date, or non-date, or whatever the hell this was.

We met Nina and West in the lobby. Lisa took her coat off. She wore some sort of red sweater that was almost long enough to be a dress. Almost, but not quite.

"What?" she said.

She'd caught me staring. Time to make a joke out of it. "Did you forget to put on pants?"

"I'm wearing leggings." She pointed at the skintight black material. "They're like pants but way more comfortable."

"We should go find seats," Nina said.

"Nope," Lisa said. "First we need popcorn."

The multiplex was pretty crowded. If we waited, we might end up in the nosebleed section. "I'll get popcorn," I offered. "You go find the seats."

"Okay."

I walked over to the concession stand, grateful there was a line because it would give me time to get my head on straight. No matter how good Lisa looked, I needed to focus on the fact that we were friends. This date wasn't real. That would be a whole lot easier to remember if she'd worn some damn pants. It felt like karma was kicking my ass, because now kissing her didn't seem like such a bad idea.

It was weird. I'd never thought of her as sexy before... She was my nerdy friend who wore sweatshirts and jeans. If she'd dressed like this when we first met, I might not have put her in the friend zone. *Huh. That's an odd thought.* I liked Lisa as a friend... It shouldn't matter what she wore.

I moved forward in line and ordered a large popcorn with extra butter because Lisa was right. Popcorn without butter tasted like Styrofoam. Once I had the popcorn and a wad of napkins, I went into the theater and looked around, trying to spot her. The theater was crowded. The previews were running, and the flickering lights made it difficult to distinguish one person from another.

I had to scan the theater a few times before I finally found her.

Chapter Eleven

Lisa

Okay. I admit it. I'd worn the sweater and leggings to torment Matt a bit. This look was outside my normal fashion comfort zone. I hadn't been lying when I said the leggings were more comfortable than pants. I'd live in these things if I could, but I'd definitely wear longer sweaters.

I was still annoyed about his behavior earlier, but the mentally healthy part of my brain said I needed to let it go. Being irritated with Matt wouldn't change him. It would just make me unhappy.

Nina led us to four seats together on the right side of the theater. I watched for Matt to come in. The theater was crowded. If he didn't come in before they dimmed the lights, he might not be able to find us. I *could* go to the lobby to meet him and lead him to our seats. Or I could let him wander around like an idiot. I was leaning toward option number two.

Matt walked in as the lights dimmed and glanced around. The flickering previews on the screen probably made it hard for him to see. I waited. When he spotted me, he smiled, and despite our recent problems, I felt myself smiling back. He crossed the theater and sat down next to me. He balanced a giant tub of popcorn on the armrest between us.

"One large popcorn with extra butter," he said.

I inhaled the buttery scent and my mouth watered. "Please tell me you remembered napkins."

"Normally I wouldn't bother. I'd just wipe my hands on my jeans." He pulled a wad of napkins from his jacket pocket. "Since you forgot to put pants on, I thought you might need these."

"Ha, ha." I leaned in so no one around us would hear. "A real boyfriend probably wouldn't gripe at his girlfriend for not wearing pants."

He chuckled at my comment and leaned back in his seat. I tuned in to the preview about people stealing cars and racing them across country. "I don't understand why that's entertaining."

"It looks awesome," Matt said.

"Such a guy movie."

Matt seemed relaxed. More like his old self. That was a relief. The most important thing about this whole situation was keeping Matt as a friend. I liked him. Liked spending time with him. I didn't want to lose that but once we dated other people how much time would we have to spend together? *Huh? That's a random thought.*

The movie started and the volume increased to a seat-shaking level. Maybe they played the movies super loud so there was no way anyone could talk during the show. I reached into the bucket of popcorn and bumped Matt's hand. I expected him to pull away from me but he didn't. He didn't even recognize the fact that our hands touched. Maybe he was finally on board with our fake dating game.

After the movie, I used the napkins Matt had given me to wipe the butter and salt from my hands. They still felt sticky. "I'm going to stop at the restroom to wash my hands."

We exited the theater and shuffled along with the crowd.

Nina and I veered off to the bathroom. As we were washing our hands, she said, "So what did Matt think of your new outfit?"

"At first he seemed confused, but then we joked about it and I think he's okay now. I hope he's done acting weird."

"He's a guy," Nina said. "They always act weird."

I laughed as we left the restrooms. Trey headed toward us with a group of artsy-looking students. He caught sight of me and grinned.

I smiled and waved. He nodded in response. "He noticed you," Nina said in a sing-song voice.

"And that is a step in the right direction." Trey noticing me gave me a small thrill. Maybe this *would* work.

We went for pizza after the movie. The Slicery was packed. We ended up sitting in a curved corner booth, which meant the four of us were squished in together on a bench seat shaped like a comma. Of course Nina and West didn't mind the close quarters. Matt and I were sitting so close our thighs touched and that was a bit awkward and distracting, especially since I wasn't wearing pants.

Matt must not have noticed because he acted like his normal self. Between bites of pepperoni pizza we talked about the movie and our plans for college.

"I'm trying to talk Charlie into going to college while I stay home and work with Dad. There's no reason for both of us to suffer through four more years of school," Matt said. "My dad built this business so he could pass it down to us. If I stayed and worked I could learn more about running the business. It's a practical solution."

"Playing devil's advocate here, but what if Charlie doesn't want to carry on the family tradition? What if he wants to do something else?"

Matt stared at me like I'd just suggested Charlie might want to major in ballroom dancing.

"What part of family business don't you understand?" he asked.

"I get it. You inherited your dad's love for fresh air and all green growing things. You know how to take care of plants and make yards look good but there's probably more to the business than that."

"Whatever it is, my dad can teach me."

I took a bite of pizza while I thought about his statement. The spicy pepperoni and stringy cheese didn't stop me from wondering why he seemed to always want to take the easy way out. Was it weird that it bothered me? If times became tough would he be the type of guy who bailed on a girl? Maybe I was lucky he'd friend-zoned me. If this is what he was really like, then keeping this relationship fake was the best way to go.

"You're judging me, aren't you?" Matt balled up a napkin and threw it at me.

"Maybe." I flicked the balled-up napkin back at him. "You're smart. I don't understand why you don't use your brain more."

"Maybe you use your brain too much. Maybe you should live in the moment and not be such a perfectionist."

"I'm not a perfectionist."

Matt looked like he was trying not to laugh.

"I'm not."

"Why do you study so much to make A's when you could relax and get a B instead?"

How could I explain? "School is a game that I'm good at. I'm not athletic or super creative, but I can study and make good grades. It's my thing."

"That is just sad," Matt teased.

"All right Mr. Judgmental, what's your thing?"

He shoved about half a piece of pizza into his mouth and chewed. Was he stalling or thinking? After swallowing, he said, "I like working with plants. I like designing layouts for people's yards and making things look better than they were before I started."

That was kind of interesting. "Do you draw things out, like an architect?"

"I have no idea what an architect does, but I can map out someone's yard and figure out what would work."

"Not to be rude, but we're on a double date which means we should talk about something together," Nina said from the other end of the booth.

"You didn't get the notes for double-dating?" Matt asked me.

"Nope. Missed those." I leaned forward so I could see Nina around Matt. "This isn't the best booth for four-way conversation, but I'll give it a shot. Pick a topic."

"Did you see that there's going to be a Harry Potter Convention in St Louis this summer? That's only a few hours away."

I sucked in a breath. "Really? We should totally go."

Matt pressed his lips together like he was trying not to laugh.

"Keep it up"—I elbowed him in the ribs—"and I'll drag you there with me."

He shook his head, but he was smiling. "It's nerdily cute."

Chapter Twelve

Matt

When I drove Lisa to her house, things between us felt much more normal than when I'd picked her up. We'd had fun at The Slicery. Even though I'd teased her about the whole Harry Potter thing, seeing her that excited was fun.

"If you were going to dress up as any Harry Potter character, who would it be?" I asked as I pulled up in front of her house.

"Not an easy question to answer. My first thought is Hermione, but I really like Luna, too."

"I think you're definitely Hermione."

"I'll take that as a compliment." She reached for the door handle and then looked at me. "This wasn't nearly as uncomfortable as I thought it would be."

"It worked out pretty good." If it were a real date, this would be the time when I would kiss her good night. My gaze drifted down to her sparkly pink lips. *Kiss her*, my gut instinct said.

"See you later." She opened the door and hopped out.

So she wasn't thinking about kissing me at all. Of course she wasn't because I'd made a scene about not wanting to kiss her. Apparently, I was an idiot.

I watched her walk up to the house and let herself in. She waved before shutting the front door. There was one thing I needed to remember. Even if I saw her as more than a friend now, she didn't want me to kiss her. She wanted Trey. And I wanted Jane. Funny, I hadn't thought about Jane once tonight.

I was watching television in the living room when Charlie came in. He grabbed a soda from the refrigerator and joined me on the couch. "So how was your double date?"

"Good."

"Uh-huh." He waited for me to say something else. I didn't.

"I don't get why you don't date her for real," Charlie said.

"You know why."

"Jane is great, but she's not available. Lisa is great, and she likes your sorry ass. Do the math."

"Wrong. Lisa likes Trey."

"She liked you first," Charlie said. "If you don't make a play for her, some other guy will."

"Whatever." I grabbed the remote and turned up the volume.

The front door opened, and Jane came in with my sister, Haley. Jane was laughing and she looked so happy. There was something about her...she always seemed so alive. Maybe I was an idiot to think she might break up with her boyfriend. But what if she did? I couldn't be dating anyone for real or I'd miss my chance. That's why this thing between Lisa and I could never be real. I wanted Jane.

"How'd your double date go?" Haley asked as she walked by.

"Good," I said.

"Lisa seems cool," Jane said. "The real test will be if you make it past the one month mark."

"What do you mean?"

"You've never been into a girl for more than a month." Jane tilted her head as she looked at me like she was questioning my intelligence. "Didn't you know that?"

"Really?" I pretended to be surprised. "I never noticed."

Jane laughed. "Maybe that should be your goal. Find someone you'll like for more than thirty days."

"Come on." Haley headed for the stairs to her bedroom and Jane followed along behind her.

"Hello, irony," Charlie muttered.

I flipped him off. He laughed.

The truth was, I'd been into Jane for several months but hadn't known how to go about asking her out since she was my little sister's best friend. It had seemed like too awkward of a line to cross. When I had finally worked up the courage to say something, she'd met Mr. Country Club and that was that. I'd missed my chance.

•••

Monday morning at school, Lisa wasn't at her locker like normal. What was that about?

"What's going on?" I asked Nina.

"What do you mean?"

Was she playing dumb? "Where's Lisa?"

"She ran to the restroom. Clingy much?"

I glared at her but didn't comment. It's not like I'd been dying to see Lisa. I wanted to move this plan along. Part of moving forward was being seen together, which was hard to do if my fake girlfriend wasn't here.

Lisa came back a few minutes later with a big grin on her face. "Good morning."

"Really?" I said. "Because it feels like your average sucky Monday to me."

She leaned in and said, "That's my normal stance on Monday, but then Trey stopped to talk to me."

Huh. That's what she was so happy about. "So the plan is working?"

"Maybe it is. He asked how I liked the movie."

"What movie?" Why did it feel like I was two steps behind in this stupid conversation?

"The movie you and I went to on Friday," she said like I was an idiot. "I saw him there and he said hello."

I nodded like I understood. "Got it." I felt the need to mention Jane like that would get my life on the right track. "Jane stayed over Friday night. She said she thinks you're cool."

"Oh," Lisa said. "I guess she noticed we're dating, too." "Yeah." I leaned against the locker. "She noticed I

never seem interested in a girl for more than a month."

"Ouch."

"Yeah, didn't make me look great." I reached up and rubbed the back of my neck.

"At least she's noticed you."

"I never realized how annoyingly optimistic you are," I said.

"I am a ray of sunshine," Lisa declared. "I bring joy and happiness wherever I go."

I laughed. "And books. Don't forget the books."

"True." She leaned her hip against the locker and

studied me. "You're not exactly a pessimist. You're just not a risk taker."

What did that mean? "Way to make me sound like a wuss."

"That wasn't an insult," she said. "Just like your study and slide routine, you seem to hold back on enthusiasm, like if you don't give something your all then you won't be disappointed if it doesn't work out."

I hated when she pulled this therapist crap on me, but she wasn't wrong. "I don't remember making an appointment, Dr. Lisa, so stop analyzing me."

"Maybe you're my pre-degree case study. If I could figure out why you act the way you do, then I could write a paper. I could call it the Boyfriend Brief."

She grinned when she said it, but it ticked me off. Maybe it was my Monday morning brain or maybe it was because the plan seemed to be working for her but not for me, but the next words out of my mouth were, "I'm not your problem to analyze and fix." I leaned in closer. "It's not like you've had a real boyfriend."

She jerked back a step and blinked her eyes really fast the way girls do when they're trying not to cry.

I rammed my hand back through my hair. "I didn't mean—"

"Forget about it. My mistake, I thought I was joking around with a friend. Not that you'd know anything about being a good friend." She turned and headed for her homeroom.

"Could you be more of a jackass?" Nina asked from where she'd been standing on Lisa's other side.

Any response I gave would only make this worse. And then West would be pissed at me for arguing with his girlfriend. I headed toward my homeroom alone.

Chapter Thirteen

Lisa

What was Matt's problem? I'd been joking. Still...his response...throwing it in my face that guys weren't lining up to date me—that had been mean.

Odds were he'd struck out at me because I'd hit too close to home. He never tried hard at anything and he had to know that was lazy. And yes, I *was* being judgmental but it was obvious he was smart. I didn't understand why he wouldn't put effort into something to get what he wanted.

You know what? Not my problem. Matt wasn't actually my boyfriend, so figuring out his personality disorder wasn't my responsibility. And for that I was grateful. At this point I wasn't sure I wanted to be his friend.

"What was Matt's deal at the lockers this morning?" Nina asked in our first hour class.

"I guess I hit a nerve."

"Since when is he so touchy?" she asked. "You guys joke around all the time."

"I guess things are different now that we're dating." Class started so our conversation ceased.

By the time lunch rolled around, I'd had about ten different imaginary conversations in my brain with Matt. Sometimes I played it cool. Sometimes I let him know he was being a tool. No matter the scenario, I kept coming back to the same thing. There was no use being upset with him because he was just a clueless guy. All of the prep made it easier for me to fake smile at him when I sat down at our lunch table.

"I thought you'd be mad at me," he said.

"No point in being mad," I said. "Because none of this is real. Right?" So much for taking the high road.

He leaned back and studied me. "There we go. That's more what I expected."

"Don't worry," I said. "Me being annoyed with you will just make our pending breakup seem more real."

"Listen, I'm sorry about what I said this morning."

"Why?"

"What do you mean, why?" He seemed genuinely confused.

"I mean, why are you sorry?"

He ran his hand back through his hair. "You ticked me off, and I said something that came out meaner than I thought it would."

"Just so you know, I had a life before we became friends." I felt the need to point this out. "I dated guys. Just because you friend-zoned me doesn't mean all guys saw me as undatable."

He nodded. "I know."

"And it's not like I've been hanging around waiting for you to ask me out. At first I thought we clicked, but then we didn't. No big deal. I moved on. I liked you as a friend. I was happy living my life in a drama-free zone." I opened my lunch bag and pulled out a bag of apple slices. "Quite honestly, it seems like I dodged a bullet."

"I like being friends with you."

"Well, you've pretty much screwed that up. Maybe we should call it quits on everything."

"I really am sorry," he said. "I was a jerk, but I think we should stick to the plan. It's working, at least for you. Trey noticed you. And maybe that's why I'm mad. This is probably going to work for you but not for me."

"Maybe you shouldn't like someone who already has a boyfriend," I said.

He just nodded. I was done talking. Even though I was trying to play it cool, this whole thing made me sick to my stomach.

After school, I headed over to Crazy Crafts. It was Monday Mask night, which meant I hosted a workshop where I helped kids create masks. We decorated them with feathers, sequins, and whatever else they wanted. I loved working with little kids because they said exactly what they meant. No guessing games required. Being around them restored my faith in humanity.

"I want more pink sequins," said a little boy wearing a Spiderman shirt.

"Pink is for girls," said the girl who happened to be hoarding all the pink sequins.

"No," I said to hoarder girl. "Pink is for whoever wants it, and we have to share the decorations."

After giving an Olympic-level eye roll, she passed him the sequins.

I was helping another little girl fashion a unicorn horn for her mask when I heard, "Hey, Lisa."

Looking up, I saw Trey walking toward me. My heart rate kicked up a notch. "Hello. Are you here to make a mask?"

"As fun as those pink sequins look, I'm actually here for paint brushes."

"Aisle four," I said.

"Cool. I was beginning to think this place only carried old-lady yarn."

"I am offended on behalf of the yarn," I said. "What does old-lady yarn mean?"

"Yarn in those Day-Glo colors that don't even exist in nature," he said.

I smiled. "I see your point. I have an afghan my grandmother made and it practically glows in the dark."

"You have cool hair," hoarder girl said to Trey.

"Thanks." Trey ran his hand back through his hair, making it look even more tussled and kind of sexy.

I shook my head. "The burden of all that coolness must be hard to bear."

"I'm up to the challenge." He grinned at me and I smiled back. "See you later." He headed toward aisle four.

"See you." I watched him walk away and sighed. Nice jeans. Cool hair. Great smile. He was the one I wanted.

Hoarder girl tapped my arm. "I want ribbons."

I tuned back in to the craft at hand and reached for a spool of hot pink curly ribbon. "Who wants curly ribbon?"

When there wasn't a blank spot left on any of the kids' masks, we put them on a drying rack and cleaned the table so we could have a snack while I waited for their parents to come sign them out.

After the last kid left, I was straightening up and getting ready to clock out when a dark-haired man with a beard approached the craft table, like he wasn't sure if he should be there.

"Can I help you?"

"Maybe." He gave a shy smile. "Are you Lisa Johnson?"

I nodded.

"Is your mother Evelyn Johnson?"

Faint alarm bells started going off in my head. Could this be one of my mom's patients? "Why do you ask?"

"I'm an old friend of your mom's," he said. "If I give you my business card, would you pass it along to her?"

No harm in that. "Sure."

The man pulled a gray card out of his wallet and set it on the table. "It was nice to meet you, Lisa." And then he turned around and left...headed straight toward the exit without buying anything...like the only reason he'd come into the store was to speak with me. Weird.

I checked out the card. Gavin Johnson. Data on Demand. Must be some type of computer tech guy.

Other people might think us having the same last name was significant but Johnson was one of the most common last names in the United States so it didn't faze me. When I was little, my mom told me there were almost two million Johnsons in America. There were times I wished I had a more unique last name but sometimes it was good to blend in.

When I walked into the house later that night, my mom sat on the couch in her Wonder Woman pj's, drinking a glass of wine and reading a book. "Hey, sweetie. How was work?"

"Good." I told her about Trey.

"He sounds like a nice guy," my mom said.

"He is. Speaking of guys." I reached into my jeans pocket and pulled out the gray business card. "Someone you used to know stopped by and gave me this." I passed it to her.

She glanced at the card and sucked in a breath. "What did he say to you?"

I told her what the man had said, word for word. "Should I be afraid? Is he some kind of stalker?"

She pressed her lips together like she wasn't sure what to say. After a moment, she shook her head no.

I waited for her to say something else. A cold sensation started in my stomach and seemed to spread outward through my body, like I just drank a large frozen Coke. "Mom?"

"Sit." She patted the seat next to her on the couch.

I sat down and waited, wondering where this was going. "Gavin was my...well, he's your father."

"What?" I practically yelled the word.

My mom nodded. "I always wondered if he'd try to come back into our lives. I figured eventually he'd want to meet you."

I laughed. "Wrong. The sperm donor didn't want to meet me. He used me to reach you."

"You don't know that," my mom said.

"He didn't even introduce himself," I reminded her.

"I can't pretend to know what he was thinking," my mom said. "But he probably looked us up online and saw where you worked and decided to visit." She glanced at the card. "He lives a few hours away in Missouri, so he put effort into driving over here."

The cold inside me changed into hot anger. "Why are you defending him?"

"I'm not—"

"He didn't want anything to do with me," I said. "He rejected me before I was born." My voice broke. My eyes burned. I was dangerously close to tears. Where in the hell was this tidal wave of emotion coming from? I took a breath and blew it out slowly. "Bottom line. He made his choice. He doesn't get another chance."

My mom moved to hug me, so I let her, but I began to feel claustrophobic. I needed to get out of the house and out of my head for a while.

Doing my best to project calm, I said, "I need to get some fresh air. I'll be back in a little bit." I grabbed my keys and headed out the front door. I dialed Nina as I climbed into my car. "Hey, this is Nina. Text me if you need me."

Crap. That meant she was with West. Who else could I talk to about this? There was only one other person I trusted, even if he did piss me off on a regular basis. I dialed Matt's number.

Chapter Fourteen

Matt

I was sitting on the couch watching *American Ninja Warrior* when my cell buzzed. Lisa's name flashed on the screen. Was she calling to gripe at me some more? I'd been a dick but then I'd apologized. There wasn't much more I could do. "Hey, Lisa. What's up?"

"I really need a friend right now. Can you forget all the weirdness that's been going on between us and just be my friend?"

"Of course."

"Can I come over?" Her voice sounded strange.

"Sure. What's wrong?"

She hung up. Crap. What was that about? She wanted me to be her friend. That was good. Still, she didn't sound happy.

I headed out onto the front porch and waited for her.

She pulled up and sat in her car with the engine running, staring at the steering wheel. I walked around the car and opened the door. "Are you okay?"

Not looking at me, she shook her head. She didn't say anything else and she didn't turn the engine off. I couldn't leave her sitting in the car. I held out my hand. "Let's go sit on the porch swing."

She turned the car off and then clasped my hand. Her gaze met mine. Red rimmed her eyes, and frustration and anger radiated off her. A desire to protect her flowed through me. I pulled her from the car and wrapped my arms around her. "How can I help?"

I could feel her take a few deep breaths like she was trying not to cry. Pushing gently against my chest, she stepped back and looked up at me. I left my arms around her because it felt right. "Okay. Long story short, my dad tracked me down and asked me to give his card to my mom."

Okay. That was out of left field. "That's weird."

"I know, right? And he didn't introduce himself or ask about me. He just acted like an old friend of my mom's. She's the one who told me who he was."

How in the hell do I deal with this? "Let's go sit on the porch swing." That would give me a few seconds to come up with something to say. Once we were seated, it felt natural to put my arm around her shoulders. She didn't seem to mind. "So you're mad because he didn't tell you who he was?"

She nodded. "It's like he just used me to get to my mom. In one way it feels like I'm overreacting, but in another way it's like he wanted nothing to do with me...again."

I knew it was just Lisa and her mom. I always thought her dad had bailed when she was a little kid. "When was the last time you saw him?"

"Never," she said. "The bastard left when he found out my mom was pregnant."

"Shit." There wasn't much else I could say. "What kind of dirtbag walks out on someone who is pregnant?"

"Exactly. My mom was so calm about the whole thing and I'm just so pissed off."

"Totally justified," I said.

Ford, our three-legged black lab, loped around the side of the house. He walked right up to us and put his head on Lisa's lap. She reached down to pet his head. "Hey, there."

"This is Ford," I said. "He doesn't like it when people are upset."

Lisa sniffled. "He'd make a good therapy dog."

She stroked Ford's ears, and I sat there with my arm around her, hoping Ford would know what to do next because I didn't have a freaking clue.

"I thought I didn't care," Lisa said. "I've known my whole life that my dad didn't want me but having him show up out of nowhere like that...not bothering to tell me who he really was...I can't explain how crazy angry I am right now. Plus I'm mad at myself for reacting this way. I should be able to blow the whole thing off."

Now was the time for me to jump in and say something to make her feel better, so I tried. "You're allowed to be mad."

"The coward should have manned up and told me who he was."

"Feel free to tell me to shut up," I said, "but maybe he didn't tell you who he was because he wanted to make sure your mom knew he was reaching out to you. Maybe he was asking her permission before he told you who he was."

Lisa glared at me.

"I still think he's a total dick, but that might have been his reason."

She nodded and continued to stroke Ford's ears. The dog sighed and closed his eyes.

"Do you think I should talk to him...give him a second chance?"

"That's up to you."

"What would you do if you were in this situation?" she asked.

That was hard to answer, because I had a great relationship with my father. "If I'd never met my dad and he showed up out of nowhere and introduced himself, I don't know how I'd act, but I definitely wouldn't be ready to forgive and forget."

"This whole situation is not helping to maintain my drama-free zone," Lisa muttered.

"Yeah, and I haven't helped with that lately. I really am sorry about being a jerk."

She looked up at me with big brown eyes. "Thank you. The good news is what you've done lately doesn't even register after meeting my dad."

Ford whined and nosed Lisa's hand.

"You stopped petting him," I said. "You aren't allowed to do that unless you give him fair warning."

Lisa laughed. "I'm sorry, Ford." Using two hands, she rubbed both of his ears at the same time. Ford made a satisfied snuffling sound.

"I think you have a new best friend."

Chapter Fifteen

Lisa

Ford snuffled and closed his eyes and the world no longer seemed like a terrible place. Maybe all I needed in my life was a dog. Having Matt's arm around me didn't hurt, either. Warmth from his body seeped into mine. "Thank you."

"For what?" Matt asked.

"For talking me off the ledge." I smiled at him. Funny how we fit together and it wasn't awkward. I couldn't help noticing that we were in the perfect position for a first kiss. If we were a real couple. But he'd gone out of his way to point out we weren't, and he had no desire to kiss me... That didn't mean he didn't care about me. Right now he was being all kinds of warm and nice and helpful.

My cell buzzed, startling me. "That's probably my mom. I left the house without telling her where I was going." I pulled my phone from my pocket and saw the text from her. "I'm making brownies. Done in twenty."

I smiled.

"Good news?" Matt asked.

"My mom always makes brownies when I'm upset. Our family motto is, *Chocolate might not fix everything but it's a good start.* I texted back that I was at Matt's and I'd be home soon.

"Your mom seems pretty cool," Matt said.

"She is. Which is another reason I can't understand why my jackass of a dad bailed."

"Sometimes people do stupid things." Matt reached over to pat Ford's head. His warm fingers brushed against mine. My heart rate kicked up a notch. The silence stretched out. Ford panted, oblivious to the tension in the air. Doggy breath drifted up to me, making me wrinkle my nose. "Ford is adorable, but he needs a mint."

Ford's ears perked up and he tilted his head, looking at me like I'd said something super interesting.

"What'd I do?" I asked Matt.

"Watch this," Matt said. "Ford, do you want a Minty?"

Ford jumped backward and did a three-legged tap dance before turning in a circle, exuding pure puppy joy.

"Come on." Matt stood and pulled me to my feet. "Watch out for Chevy. Once he hears the treat bag open, he'll come flying in here."

I followed Matt into the house. His kitchen was off to the right. He opened one of the bottom cabinets and pulled out a bag that said Minty's Dog Treats on the front. The top opened like a ziplock bag. He didn't even have the bag all the way open before another dog, also with three legs, came zooming in from another room.

Matt gave each dog a green bone, and they trotted off to lie side by side on a throw rug in the living room.

"I have two questions. First, what's in those things?" Matt grinned and tossed the bag back in the cabinet.

"Peppermint oil, parsley, and some other stuff. It really does help with their breath. I tried one once." He grimaced. "It tasted terrible."

"You tried one?" I smiled at the idea of Matt biting into a green dog treat. "Why?"

"Charlie did it first, so I kind of had to."

Guys were so weird. "That's a twin thing?"

"A brother thing," he said. "What's your second question?"

"Why do your dogs only have three legs?"

"Before we adopted them, they both had run-ins with cars."

"That's sad."

"Yeah. My sister Haley volunteers at an animal shelter, and she agreed to foster them during their recovery."

"And then you fell in love and never gave them back?" I guessed.

"Pretty much."

"And their names?"

"Kind of an inside joke," Matt said. "Ford's name at the shelter was something ridiculous like Francis."

"Ford seems to fit him better." I caught sight of the clock on the wall behind him. It had been twenty minutes since my mom texted. "I think those brownies are done so I better go. Thanks for helping with my mental breakdown."

He leaned back against the counter with his hands in his front jeans pockets. "No problem. That's what friends are for," he said. "And no matter what stupid things I say, I'll always be your friend."

"Thanks. And I'll try not to get mad when you say dumb things because you are a good friend."

"Gee, thanks."

I grinned, feeling the balance of the universe had been restored. "See you tomorrow." I didn't wait for him to offer to walk me out to my car, because I was pretty sure he wasn't going to and that could have been awkward anyway. As I drove home, my traitorous brain replayed the way he'd hugged me and put his arm around me on the swing. He was a good guy. He just wasn't the guy for me. I needed to keep my eyes on the prize...focus on Trey or on making myself appear datable. In a few weeks, Matt and I would be firmly back in the friend zone where we belonged.

When I walked into the house the mouthwatering scent of chocolate filled the air. I headed straight for the kitchen where my mom sat at the table halfway through her brownie. "Hey, sweetie. Feeling better?"

"Yes, and no." I cut myself a hunk of brownie and joined my mom at the table. Before hashing this out, I took a bite. Warm gooey chocolate goodness made the world seem like a better place. Fortified with chocolate, I was ready to share. I told Mom about how Matt had acted.

"So he was good to you and then he reminded you that he isn't boyfriend material?" my mom said.

"No." I hadn't seen it that way. "I'm pretty sure he is boyfriend material. He doesn't see *me* as girlfriend material."

"But you went to the movies last weekend." She cut herself another piece of brownie. "I don't understand why he's backpedaling."

Should I tell my mom about my secret agreement with Matt? I trusted her not to share, so I dove in. "Here's the thing." I filled her in on my fake-dating deal and our theory about the wedding ring effect.

She sat back and crossed her arms over her chest and gave me the mother of all mom-looks.

"Wow. That is not a look of approval."

"No. It's not. Matt is going after someone who is in a committed relationship. That's wrong."

I squirmed in my seat. "I don't think he's going after her. It's more like he wants her to see that he isn't just Haley's older brother. He's someone that could be a good boyfriend if she is ever single again. And I'd like to add that the person whose attention I want isn't dating anyone."

"I still say Matt is in denial. He better figure out what he wants or you'll end up with Trey and he'll end up by himself." She took a deep breath. "Can we talk about Gavin? You have every right to be upset, but I need to know how you're feeling."

"Blindsided," I said. "And angry and confused and just...sad."

"Understandable." She took another bite of brownie. "I'm feeling mostly angry that he approached you. He should have contacted me first."

"Yes, he should have," I said. "What are you going to do about him?"

"I'm not sure. Now that he's here, he probably won't go away, so I'll call him in a few days and see what he wants."

"Is it wrong that part of me hopes he's contacted us because he's dying of some terribly painful disease?" I was only sort of joking.

"That's a little bit wrong," my mom said. "There was a time where I would have gladly mowed him down with my car and shown zero remorse. Since then, I've realized I wasn't the problem. He's the one with issues."

"So you no longer want to run him over?"

"Maybe with a small scooter or a bike," my mom said. "Nothing that would cause any permanent damage."

I laughed.

Chapter Sixteen

Matt

After Lisa left, I stood there feeling confused. When she'd shown up in tears, all I'd wanted to do was take care of her. Once I had my arm around her on the porch swing, I hadn't wanted to let go. It would be easy to just go with this, but in the end it wouldn't work because she'd never be Jane and I'd never be Trey.

Chevy barked at me. "What?"

He hopped up and trotted over to the cabinet where we kept the dog treats.

"You had one," I said.

He sat down and tilted his head, staring at me with big puppy dog eyes. He glanced back at the cabinet door, thumped his tail on the floor, and gave a small whine.

"Fine." I grabbed two more dog treats and passed them out. "Last one," I warned.

"They never believe that," Charlie said as he came down the stairs into the living room. "What was up with Lisa?"

How much should I share? "Rough day. Family drama."

"And she came to you because you're her—"

"Friend," I said.

"Right."

"Shut up."

●●●

Tuesday morning, Lisa acted normal at her locker and at lunch. I didn't mention anything about any of the drama from yesterday and neither did she. Good. I'd been worried about nothing. Our fake dating plans were still on track.

Wednesday on the way into the building my grand plan went right off the rails when I saw what Lisa was wearing. It was just a dress with some crazy pattern, but it emphasized her curves and had me thinking non-friend thoughts. And damn it all if Trey wasn't standing there next to her car talking to her and leaning in a little too close to a girl who was supposed to have a boyfriend. What did she see in that guy besides his weird hair? And why did I want to punch him? I had no reason to be mad. This was a good thing. Maybe I wanted to punch him because of his stupid hair.

As I approached, Lisa glanced up and spotted me. She didn't acknowledge me, just went back to her conversation. I wanted to stop and interrupt them, but that wasn't part of the plan, so I cut between rows of cars and headed toward the front entrance.

Nina and West were already at her locker.

"Why do you look so annoyed?" Nina asked.

"It's morning and I'm awake."

"There's this fabulous thing called caffeine," Nina said. "It comes in convenient tea and coffee form."

I didn't bother responding.

Right before the bell rang, Lisa came down the hall with a big grin on her face. "Good morning."

"Morning," I shot back. So far there hadn't been much good about it.

"Thanks for not interrupting when I was talking to Trey."

"How'd that go?" I asked, pretending I cared.

"Pretty good. I think there's a fifty percent chance he'll ask me out when we break up."

I nodded like that was a good thing.

"Any news on the Jane front?"

"No."

"As a friend, I'm going to suggest it might be time to concentrate on someone else. I know she's who you really want, but she might never be available. There are a lot of nice, cool girls out there. Maybe you should look for a new one."

At lunch West said, "Don't forget it's my mom's birthday this weekend, and I expect both of you to be there."

"You're having a party at your house?" Lisa said. "I didn't think your dad was a people person."

"He's not. But he likes to have family over for birthdays...outside in the backyard," West said. "Matt is family. You're his girlfriend. So you get to enjoy an awkward gathering in our yard."

"Don't worry," I said to Lisa. "You're not going."

"Oh," Lisa said. "*Okay.*"

Crap. "I mean you can come if you want."

"Remember when you agreed to stop doing weird things that annoyed me? You're not holding up your end of the bargain."

I laughed. "Believe me, you don't want to go. This party won't be fun. I was trying to save you the trouble."

"Wow," Nina said. "Rude much?"

I pointed at West. "Do you think your mom's birthday party is going to be fun or will it be stressful and awkward for everyone?"

"I'm going with the second answer," West said.

"So there's no reason for you to go," I told Lisa. "Plus if I don't take a date I can leave earlier. It's a win-win. Understand?"

She nodded, but she didn't look happy about it.

The bell rang, signaling the end of lunch. I watched as Lisa stood and walked off. Why did it feel like I was suddenly in a lose-lose situation?

For the rest of the day, I tried to forget about Lisa and focus on Jane. There was one major flaw with this plan. Whenever I saw Jane she was with her perfect boyfriend. Maybe I was an idiot. Maybe Lisa was right. Maybe I did need to find a new girl to concentrate on. What kind of girl did I want?

I kept my eyes open for any possible candidates. There wasn't a shortage of cute girls but there did seem to be a shortage of girls who were interesting. And it's not like I could flirt with other girls while I was fake dating Lisa because that would make me look like a jerk.

•••

After school, I stacked bags of mulch for my dad, staggering them at right angles to make a zig zag pattern in front of the checkout area by the decorative planters.

My dad came up from the greenhouses to check on my progress. "Huh." He rubbed his chin. "Looks a lot better than the way I would have done it."

"Interesting is always better," I said.

"Like Jane?" my dad said.

I stopped mid-stride. "What?"

"I'm not blind," he said. "But Lisa seems interesting, too."

I set the bag of mulch down. "Has Charlie been running his mouth?"

He grinned. "A little bit. So, about Lisa?"

I wiped sweat off my forehead. "She's interesting, too."

"Then you need to figure out what you want."

"That's the problem." I grabbed a bag of mulch and started another stack. "I thought I knew what I wanted, but now I'm not sure."

"When it's right, you'll know."

"How'd you know?" As far as I knew, he and my mom got together in high school and that was it.

"You can't repeat this," my dad said. "Women go on and on about soul mates or finding that one person you can't live without. For guys it's not about finding someone you can't live without. It's more like you can't live with the idea of her with anyone else. The idea of your mom with anyone else made me crazy, so I knew she was the one."

That made sense, sort of.

He grinned. "You've seen Jane with someone else and it's bothered you, but not like I'm talking about. If you saw Lisa with someone, how would you feel?"

Huh. I'd seen Lisa with Trey. "I've seen her with someone else, and it's pissed me off."

"Maybe that's a sign." My dad smacked me on the shoulder. "Those are all the words of wisdom I have to share."

I nodded and went back to stacking the mulch. If Lisa and Trey got together, how would I feel about it? My stomach twisted. Then again, it was almost time for dinner. I was probably just hungry.

Chapter Seventeen

Lisa

Wednesday morning I stared into my closet at my limited options and yawned. I should've done some laundry last night.

My mom came into my room and laughed. "I just spent ten minutes making that exact same face at the clothes hanging in my closet." She peered over my shoulder. "We need a house elf."

I laughed. "An emancipated house elf who works because he wants to, right?"

"Of course." She reached into my closet and grabbed a black sweater. "I'm stealing this. Feel free to raid my closet."

"Okay." I headed for her room and flipped through a couple of button-down blouses I had no desire to wear. There was a black and white flannel shirt that looked comfortable. I reached for it and hesitated. And that was ridiculous. I would not base my wardrobe on what some guy might like. I'd be myself and wear what I wanted to be happy and comfortable and hope that I came off looking cute in the process. It's not like Trey would stop talking to me because I wore something he didn't like.

I ended up wearing leggings and combat boots with the flannel shirt. Comfortable and sort of stylish. Maybe I'd start a new trend, call it nerd-girl chic.

My mom was filling a blue travel cup with coffee when I walked into the kitchen. I yawned and grabbed the bag of wheat bread from the pantry and slid two slices into the toaster. "Why are weeks so long and weekends so short?"

"Good question."

"Can we talk to someone about making three-day weekends the norm?"

"When I am queen, all weekends shall be three days long. Until then, we'll just have to deal." She grabbed her keys off the counter. "I'll see you tonight. Tony is joining us for dinner."

"Sounds good."

I made it to school a little later than normal. Matt stood at my locker staring off into space. Nina and West were holding hands and talking with their faces close together. Were they being romantic or were they plotting something? When it came to my best friend, it was hard to tell.

I waved my arms when I was within a foot of Matt, causing him to tune back into the world. He blinked and gave a slight smile. "Hello."

"Hey." I yawned wide enough for him to see my molars.

He grinned. "That's exactly how I feel right now."

I leaned against the lockers and smiled up at him. "I'm telling myself the weekend isn't that far away. The day after tomorrow is Friday."

"That's normally how weeks work," Matt said. "Let me guess. You're already plotting what books you want to hunt for with Nina."

"Of course I am. It's a sacred nerd-girl tradition. You could join us if you like. I could explain the best way to stalk the clearance section."

"Hard to resist such an exciting offer, but no."

"Your loss." I wondered if Matt would mention the birthday party at West's house because despite what he said, I kind of wanted to go. Minutes ticked by, and he didn't bring it up. Then again he didn't say much of anything. I couldn't figure out if I should be annoyed or grateful.

After school, Nina and I went to hang out at Great Grounds for coffee and a cookie.

"How much longer are you and Matt going to keep doing this?" Nina asked.

I stirred French vanilla creamer into my coffee. "I don't know. I told him I'd give him three weeks, and then we'd re-evaluate the situation. So if we stick with that plan, our deal ends a week from next Saturday."

"And then?"

"That is the million-dollar question," I said. "Trey is talking to me, but he talks to a lot of other girls, too."

"Next question. Is part of you hoping that Matt will ask you to the birthday party?" Nina broke the flower-shaped sugar cookie in half and passed me my portion.

"It's not like I'm dying to stand around in West's backyard making awkward small talk with his mom." According to Nina, the woman was a hoarder and practically a shut-in. She came outside and sat at the patio table in their backyard, but that was about it. "No matter how bad the party might be, having someone there that you like and had fun with would make it more tolerable. Right?"

Nina nodded. "That's how I see it."

"I guess Matt would rather leave early than make the best of a bad situation. Is it me, or does his answer to everything seem to be bailing?"

"He does seem to take the easy way out. Since that's the case, are you still interested in him?"

I took a bite of the cookie while I considered her question. Was I still interested? "I'm not sure. When I needed him, he was there for me, but he also does things that piss me off on a regular basis."

"Maybe you should aim for a seventy to thirty percent ratio of good versus annoying behavior."

"Why can't I aim for zero annoying behavior?"

"I don't think life works that way. Enough talk about guys. There's a fundraiser for the library coming up. Do you want to help me figure out what we can donate?"

"Sure." Anything to do with books was always a worthy cause. Our local library had closed because the building was falling apart and there wasn't enough money to fix it. The town was in the process of raising funds to build a new one. In the meantime, we had a tiny free library that West had helped set up as a gift to Nina. It had been a great romantic gesture. I needed a guy like that. Someone who would go out of his way to show he liked me. Not that I needed a giant romantic gesture, but it would be nice to know someone actually wanted to be with me. Not that he wanted me because he couldn't have his first choice or because I was the nearest available female.

"With Easter coming up," Nina said, "I think we could make some book-themed baskets."

"Will there be chocolate in the baskets? Because anything that claims to be Easter-related should have some form of candy."

"Chocolate could get on the books. We'd be better off going with jelly beans."

"Sad but true." I wasn't a fan of jelly beans. I hated the feeling of biting into the sugar coating. "I can see if Crazy Crafts will donate some baskets and ribbons."

"I was hoping you'd say that. You're my craft connection."

Chapter Eighteen

Matt

Friday morning, I woke up with a start when the alarm on my cell went off. I reached up to rub the back of my neck. Why did I feel like crap?

And then it came back to me. I'd had weird dreams all night. I was trying to pick Lisa up for a date. When I went to start the truck, the key broke off in the ignition. After I finally dug the half-key out with some needle nose pliers, I couldn't find another set of keys because Charlie had them. I tracked him down at Clarissa's house. He gave me the keys and I was able to start the truck except I only made it to the end of the driveway before it sputtered and died because the gas gauge was on empty. When I tried to fill the tank with gas we kept on hand for the lawn mower, I somehow set the truck on fire. My dad and Charlie stood off to the side, watching as the truck burned. My dad said, "You did this to yourself. No point in regretting it now."

I'd grabbed a hose and tried to put out the fire, but wherever the water hit, the flames grew brighter, like I was spraying kerosene instead of water. The flames crawled toward the house. And then Trey showed up with Lisa. With a flip of his magic hair, he put out the fire and then he rode off into the sunset with Lisa on a freaking horse.

What in the hell was my brain trying to do to me? Magic hair? A horse? I would have called in sick and stayed home to sleep if I wasn't scared about what my brain would throw at me next.

"What's your problem?" Charlie asked at breakfast.

I relayed the dream to him, including all the weird details.

He laughed. "Dude, that's funny."

It hadn't felt funny at the time. "What do you think it means?"

"It means you should ask Lisa out for real before she breaks up with you and moves on to the dude with the magic hair."

Maybe he wasn't wrong. I poured more Cap'n Crunch into my cereal bowl. "I'm thinking about it."

"What do you mean ask Lisa out for real?" our sister Haley said as she walked into the kitchen.

Shit. I needed to say something but my brain wasn't up to speed. I sighed and rubbed my temples. "It means we're kind of dating to see if it works."

"Isn't that how everyone dates?" Haley asked.

"Smart. Ass. When I asked her out, we talked about how we wanted to stay friends if it didn't work. So we agreed to date for a while and then if it didn't work we'd go back to the friend zone."

"That makes sense," Haley said. "It doesn't have a chance in hell of working, but it makes sense."

"Why wouldn't it work?"

"If only one of you wants to go back to being friends, how do you think the other person is going to feel?"

"Not happy, and I get that. But listen, don't tell anyone about this. Not even Jane." *Especially not Jane.* "I promised Lisa I wouldn't tell."

"Fine, I'll just make a mental note in case I need blackmailing material later." She grabbed a granola bar and headed back upstairs.

Well, shit. "Do you think she'll tell Jane?"

Charlie shrugged. "Not sure that it will matter if she does, since Jane is dating Mr. Perfect."

Like I needed him to throw that in my face. "Shut up."

"Just stating the obvious," he said.

...

I met up with Lisa at our lockers. Maybe we needed to talk this out.

"We made it through our first week," Lisa said like she was happy about that fact.

Was she happy we'd been able to keep up the pretense of dating, or happy one week was over and she'd be free to move on soon? I said what I knew she wanted to hear. "Two more to go, and then we'll see how things are going for you and Trey."

"What about you and you-know-who?" she whispered like she was some sort of undercover spy.

"Voldemort isn't really my type," I joked.

She laughed and then in an unexpected move, she hugged me.

I hugged her back. "What was that for?"

"You made a Harry Potter joke. That's the first time I've ever heard you do that."

"Oh no," I said. "You must have infected me with nerd-girl germs."

"Maybe." She rocked forward on the balls of her feet. "Or you could be evolving into a Harry Potter fan."

"I saw the movie," I said. "I didn't read the book."

"You left plural endings off of both of those words"

"What?"

"Movies and books. More than one in both series."

"Well I've seen the first movie, so I have the basics down."

"You realize now it's my duty, as a member of the Harry Potter fandom, to make sure you watch the other movies. I mean the books are better, but I can't see you committing to reading that many pages, so we'll start with the movies."

Her eyes were bright and she seemed to radiate enthusiasm. "Sure. I'd love to do that. But, darn it, the movies aren't playing in the theaters anymore."

"I own all of them," she said. "I think that's what we should do Saturday night. Have a Harry Potter movie marathon."

"*Uhm...*" I had no real desire to watch those movies, but Lisa looked so excited about it. "Okay, but I expect popcorn."

"I can handle that." And then her smile faded. "Crap, you're supposed to go to West's mom's party on Saturday."

That was at one. I'd have plenty of time to go over to Lisa's house afterward. But I could see the way she was looking at me...sort of hopeful. I knew what I needed to do. "We could go to West's together and then go watch movies...if you want."

Her face brightened. "Sure. That sounds good."

As we walked to homeroom, I rolled one question around in my brain. *Am I a total sucker?*

By lunchtime I questioned my sanity. Why had I asked her to go to what would be a boring and uncomfortable family event? I'm sure Nina had filled her in on my aunt's strange ways, but knowing about it didn't make it less awkward.

"Any ground rules I should know about your mom's birthday party?" Lisa asked West. He knew Lisa was clued into his mom's issues, but I wasn't sure if his parents knew anyone besides family was aware of the situation. "We're using the bathroom next door at Nina's house since my dad is still remodeling ours and it's a mess."

West said this with complete sincerity. He'd been lying to cover up for his mom's hoarding for so long it must be second nature.

"I can deal with that," Lisa said, like she believed him.

Chapter Nineteen

Lisa

As I was getting ready for my date with Matt...wait...not a date...a fake date...just hanging out with a friend...that's how I needed to think about it. Anyway, as I was trying not to stab myself in the eye with my mascara wand, I ran down the list of items my mom had brought home from the store for my not-a-date. We had cheese popcorn, caramel popcorn, regular popcorn, iced tea, and lemonade. Sometimes my mom liked to go overboard in the preparedness department. Regular popcorn would've been fine.

I checked my cell. Matt was due to pick me up in fifteen minutes. Why hadn't I gotten ready earlier? I had, but the getting ready portion of the day had included a marathon session of laundry followed by me trying on four different tops before switching back to the first one I'd planned on wearing. Not sure why I was nervous. This wasn't a date...*wasn't a date...wasn't a date.* Maybe if I chanted that in my head I'd believe it. My body ignored the message as butterflies fluttered around in my stomach.

I wasn't excited about Matt. I was excited about cake and then Harry Potter. Yes. That was it. West wasn't the only one who was good at lying.

A knock sounded on the front door. I ran to answer it, yanked open the door with a smile on my face, and then I froze. Talk about an unwelcome surprise. It wasn't Matt. It was Gavin, the sperm donor. "What the hell are you doing here?" may not have been the most polite greeting, but those are the words that flew out of my mouth, and I didn't regret them.

Gavin took a step back. "So...this is a bad time?"

Matt pulled up to the curb and parked. He came toward me smiling, and then he saw the look on my face. "What's wrong?" He looked at Gavin like he was trying to figure the situation out.

"Mom," I yelled. "You have an unwelcome guest."

Mom came to the door and frowned when she saw who was on our doorstep. "Gavin, what are you doing here?"

"I got your message," he said, "so I thought I'd stop by."

"You thought wrong," I said.

"Lisa, why don't you and Matt go to your party." Mom put her hand on my shoulder. "I can handle this."

I glanced at Gavin and then back at her. "We'll wait in the truck until he leaves."

Gavin laughed like I was joking, but I wasn't. I followed Matt to his truck and climbed in when he opened the door. Once he was in the driver's seat, he said, "Sperm donor?"

"Yep."

"And he just dropped by like he thought that was okay."

"Yep."

"Seems like a dick."

"Yep." I sat and watched as Gavin spoke to my mom. No way were we leaving until he was gone. Even then I wasn't sure I wanted to leave her alone. Tony worked tonight. I didn't like the idea of her being in the house by herself now that Gavin knew where we lived.

"Your mom looks like she's handling the situation pretty good," Matt said. "But I'd be happy to punch the guy."

"I'd be happy for you to punch him, too, but my mother would not approve."

"Too bad."

I sat and watched for a few more minutes until Gavin turned and headed for his car. Once he pulled away, I hopped out and headed back up to the front door. Matt followed. My mom stepped back to let us both inside.

"What was that about?" I asked.

She sighed. "I called and left a message, but instead of returning my call he decided to drop by."

"Why would he think we'd be all right with that?"

"I guess my message was too nice." She sat on the couch. "I think I might still hate him. And that's not healthy."

"Sounds normal to me." I sat next to her and waited to see what else she'd say.

"I told him he should call tomorrow and we could set up a time to meet that works for all of us."

"*Umm*...I hate that idea."

She laughed. "Me too, but if we don't set something up he'll keep dropping by. He says he has something he needs to say and he wants to give you something."

"He can take whatever it is and shove it up his—"

"Lisa," my mom warned before I could finish my

heartfelt sentence.

"Fine."

"You two should go to your party," she said. "I'm going to read and have a glass of wine."

"You sure?"

She nodded.

"Okay."

Matt and I headed out to the car. "And you thought West's was going to be the awkward part of the day."

Matt laughed. "Just wait."

Thirty minutes later, I sat at a picnic table in West's backyard, eating cake and wishing I'd stayed home. West's dad looked like he had zero desire to be at his own wife's party. His mom looked like she was listening to voices the rest of us couldn't hear. Everyone else seemed to be working at pretending everything was normal and we were all having a good time.

I leaned close to Matt. "You're right. This is bad."

"Told you," he said. "The good news is we only need

to stay about twenty minutes longer. Then we can go binge watch Harry Potter."

"Best news I've heard all day."

Twenty minutes later, West's dad started cleaning up everyone's plates whether they were done with them or not. "Thank you all for coming."

There were choruses of "Thanks for inviting us" and "Happy Birthday" and then everyone dispersed like they were fleeing for their lives.

"What the heck was that about?" I asked Matt as we

walked back to his truck.

"My uncle can only do about an hour of being social and then he's done."

"That's funny but sad," I said.

Matt started the truck. "We're all used to it."

"Your dad isn't like that, is he?"

"No. He's not a people person and he'd rather work with plants, but he can carry on a conversation."

When we made it back to my house, we walked through the living room into the kitchen, looking for my mom. She was sitting on the back patio. She glanced up from her book when we came outside. "That was fast."

"Not fast enough," I said.

"I warned you," Matt muttered.

"Anyway," I said, ignoring his jab, "we're going to set up the Harry Potter movie marathon downstairs."

"Have fun."

I couldn't wait to see what he thought of the basement. The entrance was off the kitchen, through a small pantry. "It has its own secret door."

"That's weird." Matt walked through what was little more than a closet and followed me down the stairs. Once he could see the room, he started laughing. "Help, I'm trapped in a bookworm's secret lair."

"I think of it as Nerd-girl Nirvana." My mom and I had hung the Hogwarts house banners on the wall behind the couch. A set of Harry Potter hardback books were displayed on a shelf between Tardis and Dalek bookends. A copy of the Marauder's Map hung on the back wall next to a pair of lightsabers. A slightly crooked floor-to-ceiling bookshelf took up the rest of the wall space.

Matt pointed at the bookshelf. "Is it supposed to lean like that?"

"It took my mom and me six hours to put that beast together. When something is advertised as 'some assembly required' it's a big fat lie. We had two wooden slats and half a dozen screws left over when we were done. It was straight when we finished. Since then, it's started to drift."

Matt rubbed his chin. "I wonder if those slats were meant to stabilize it."

"Probably," I said. "But there wasn't a chance in hell we were going to take it apart and start over."

He nodded. "If I need help building something I won't call you."

Chapter Twenty

Matt

Lisa picked up the TV remote and said, "Have a seat and I'll get this started."

"I already saw the first one," I reminded her. Seeing her this excited was entertaining, but there was no way I was sitting through all of the Harry Potter movies.

She clutched the remote control to her heart. "Even though it goes against my nerd-girl instincts, I guess we can start with the second one." She pulled up the movie on her DVR. "Before we start, do you want popcorn and a drink?" We'd just eaten cake at the birthday party from hell.

"I'm good. Maybe later."

She came and sat next to me on the couch. Just like the furniture upstairs, it was small, so there wasn't a lot of room between us. Once she hit play, she kept her eyes glued to the screen. I watched her almost more than I did the movie.

She really was cute. If this were a real date, I'd put my arm around her, but since it wasn't, I kept my arm planted by my side. Twice, I almost put my arm around her shoulders out of instinct, but I stopped myself. What was I thinking? This was Lisa. Not a real date. That might be easier to remember if she didn't smell good and have curves in all the right places.

When the movie ended, she turned to me with a huge grin on her face. "What did you think?"

"It was pretty good," I said. "The flying car was cool and I liked the whomping willow. If they were real, my dad could sell those like crazy."

"You could plant them as a security system," she said. "Do you want something to drink now?"

"Yeah." And I needed to get out of there before I gave in and pulled her close. "I might need to get out of the basement for a little bit. It's starting to close in on me."

"One of the benefits of being short is you never feel claustrophobic in small spaces." She stood. "We can go sit outside on the patio."

"Sounds good." I followed her upstairs, trying to ignore the way her jeans emphasized her curves. This wasn't a date. I needed to remember that.

We walked back into the weird pantry and through the next doorway into the kitchen. "It's almost like someone wanted to keep the basement hidden."

"Maybe the guy who built the house wanted it as his secret underground hideaway." She grabbed two glasses from the cabinet above the dishwasher. "Is lemonade okay?"

"Sure." I walked over to the sliding glass patio doors and flipped the latch. I tried to slide the door open, but it only moved about an inch before coming to an arm-jarring stop. I checked the track. What looked like a broom handle kept the door from opening. "Is this your high tech security system?"

"Not as fun as a whomping willow, but it works."

I picked up the broom handle. Now what? I glanced around.

"Just stand it up in the track," Lisa said.

"Has it ever fallen over and locked you out?" I asked. "No, but now that you mentioned it you probably jinxed us so set it on the kitchen table instead."

Once we were outside, I took a deep breath of fresh air. "I swear you're part plant," Lisa said. "You always look so relieved when you come outside."

"As long as the weather is nice, outside is always better than inside," I said.

"Personally, I prefer air conditioning and a bug-free zone."

"You do realize you're a lot bigger than any bug. And they're more afraid of you than you are of them."

"Yeah, that argument never made much sense to me. Spiders may be small but they have venom and fangs and they're just creepy."

I laughed. "I bet you love when all those Halloween spider decorations are on sale at Crazy Crafts."

"I hate those things. Some kid spilled a bag of rubber spiders all over the store. I kept finding them. One time I bent down to pick one up, and it crawled up my finger. I was not amused."

"Did you scream?"

"Loudly. After that, I had a stomp first and then check for signs of life policy."

I tried not to laugh but I couldn't help it. "I don't suppose any cameras in the store recorded security footage of that event?"

"No, thank goodness." She sipped her lemonade.

And she looked cute doing it. *What is wrong with me?* It was a good thing I wasn't sitting right next to her any longer. Out here, sitting on opposite sides of the patio table, it was easier to remember I wasn't supposed to put a move on her.

"So, should we plan anything interesting for our second week of fake dating?" I asked.

The corners of her mouth turned down. "I hadn't really thought about it and I don't like feeling that there's a countdown until this experiment fails."

"Trey has noticed you," I said. "So you're doing better than I am."

Lisa wiped condensation off of her glass. "What is it about Jane? Why do you like her?"

Huh. How could I explain my crush? "She's quirky and funny and she always does something unexpected."

"So you want someone who is unpredictable?"

"I guess. She also always makes me laugh."

Lisa narrowed her eyes. "The fact that she's a cute blonde doesn't hurt, either, does it?"

"No. What about you? Why Trey?"

She shrugged. "He's cute and funny and I feel like I don't have to act a certain way around him. I can be whoever I want to be because he doesn't have any expectations."

I rolled my eyes. "Yeah. Right. Do you think he'll be cool with your Harry Potter obsession, or your love of all things books?"

She squirmed in her chair. "You don't think he'd be okay with that?"

"With his hair and the ripped jeans, he's trying really hard to be cool, so I don't know if he'd be into the whole nerd-girl vibe you have going on." She looked upset. Time to backpedal. "I think it's cute, but he may be too cool to deal with it."

"It's not like I'm nerdy all the time," she protested.

I sipped my lemonade to keep from laughing.

"What?"

"You wear Harry Potter socks."

"Not every day."

"How many pairs do you own?" I asked.

She looked off to the side like she was thinking. "I may or may not own fourteen pairs of ultra-cool, super hip, devastatingly sexy Harry Potter socks."

"Well, if you're trying to attract Mr. Cool, you might want to stick with regular socks for a while."

"I shouldn't have to change what I do to date someone," she said.

"If the guy you want to date is shallow enough and cares that much about being cool, then you probably would have to suppress some of your nerdiness."

"You're being awful judgmental when you don't even know the guy." Lisa crossed her arms over her chest.

"I'm just calling it like I see it. Anyone who spends that much time on his hair is way too concerned with appearances."

"It's not like you walk out of the house with bedhead,"
she countered.

I reached up and ran my hand through my hair. "This is air dried, rarely brushed, and it's good enough."

Chapter Twenty-One

Lisa

"Not everyone can have naturally wavy hair that falls into place," I said.

"That's not the point. The point is, he probably spends more time on his hair than you do."

I paused in confusion. "So are you saying you think he spends too much time on his hair or I need to spend more time on my appearance?"

"The first one," Matt said.

If I wasn't trying to date Trey, would Matt be so annoyed by him? Who knew? He probably wasn't wrong about the socks, though. I could tone my nerdiness down a little bit until Trey and I knew each other better. Everyone acted on their best behavior in the beginning of relationships...right? Here I was thinking about a fantasy relationship rather than paying attention to the friend I was spending time with. "Let's stop talking about Trey and Jane and just have fun as friends, okay?"

He nodded, but he seemed annoyed.

"I work tomorrow," I said to get the conversational ball rolling again.

"Me too. I'm supposed to be done by noon but my dad doesn't really pay attention to the clock, just what needs to be done."

"Is it weird working for your dad?" I loved my mom but I couldn't imagine working with her.

"No. I mean, there's no way to call in sick and play hooky since I live with my boss, but other than that, it's good."

Talking about his dad made me think of my dad. "I can't believe Gavin stopped by like that today."

"Maybe your mom should set up an appointment for him to visit so you can get it over with."

"You might be right."

"Do you know what you want to say to him?"

I drew a line in the condensation my glass had left on the table. "I used to have this whole speech prepared. Things I'd say to him to make him regret missing out on being part of our family. Then I grew up and realized he opted out...he made his choice. Now I don't want to say much of anything to him except to tell him to go to hell."

"Sounds about right." He finished off his lemonade. We talked about less serious things and then he left. Maybe we'd watch the rest of the Harry Potter movies another day.

•••

Working Sunday mornings kind of sucked but it wasn't hard.

Today I was teaching little kids how to make a potholder with a loom. Not that difficult. Their parents could have read the directions and explained it to them in fifteen minutes. Sometimes parents used our classes for babysitting while they ran errands or wandered around the store looking for their own projects, which was kind of smart and kind of lazy at the same time. Then again, who was I to judge? If the kids were happy and the parents had a few minutes to themselves, it was a win-win.

I had four eight-year-old girls on a play date. Three of them were into the pot holders but one had zero interest.

"Would you like to color?" I offered the odd-girl-out some markers and a couple of coloring sheets.

"Yes." She smiled and picked out a Minions scene.

Problem solved. Why couldn't all predicaments be settled so easily? I sat back and watched the girls as they wove the stretchy bands of fabric through one another.

Out of the corner of my eye, I saw a familiar face. Matt came down the aisle toward me. What was he doing here?

"Hey, there," he said.

"Hello."

He picked up one of the stretchy fabric bands from the potholder kit. "What's this about?"

"Potholders." I held up the extra loom the little girl hadn't been interested in. "I have a spare loom if you feel like making one."

"Maybe next time." He tossed the piece of fabric back on the table. "How much longer until you're off work?"

I checked the clock on the back wall. "The potholder party is over in fifteen minutes and then I'm free to go."

"Cool. I'll be back." He walked away like it was normal for him to show up where I worked.

"He's cute," said the little girl who'd opted to color.

"Yes, he is," I agreed.

"Is he your boyfriend?" she asked.

"Sort of."

"What does that mean?" she asked.

"It means guys are complicated."

"My brother is just obnoxious," she said. I laughed.

Fifteen minutes later, the girls had finished their projects, their moms had paid, and I was officially done for the day.

I was cleaning up the craft table when Matt headed down the aisle carrying a bag.

"All done?" he asked. I nodded.

"Cool. It's beautiful outside. Do you want to go to the park?"

I had no idea what was going on but I would go with it. "Sure."

Matt seemed to be in a good mood. The way he was behaving, this seemed real. Like he was there to see *me* and spend time with me, not because he was acting. A part of me wished that were true, but if he'd been interested, he'd had a long time to act on it and he hadn't. Maybe he was just playing a role and hoping it would get back to Jane that he was boyfriend material. Then again, maybe he was just being a friend.

Whatever, I should enjoy this day with him and not question his motives. When we made it to the parking lot, I veered left and headed for my car.

"What are you doing?" he asked.

"I drove to work." Which in my mind meant I'd drive wherever we were headed and meet him there.

"I'll bring you back to your car," he said.

"Oh, okay." I climbed up into his truck and buckled my seat belt. He had the windows down so fresh air was streaming in and blowing my ponytail all over the place.

I hit the button to raise my window a little bit.

"Wimp," Matt teased.

"Hey," I laughed and whacked him on the arm. "You don't have hair to blow all over the place."

He grinned but didn't say anything else. Once we reached the park Matt found a spot for his truck and said, "Want to walk the trail?"

"Sure." And then I realized there was one small problem. "My jacket is in my car." The sun was shining, but it was sixty degrees and windy as heck.

Matt reached into the small backseat of the truck. "One of the benefits of dating a landscaper." He held out a hoodie that said *Patterson Landscaping* across the back. "The fashionable clothing."

"That will work." I climbed out of the car and shrugged the hoodie on. It smelled like Matt...sort of a mix between fresh green growing things and Ivory soap and it came down to mid-thigh.

Matt came around the truck. "You'll start a new trend." We headed for the trail that went around the lake. People were playing Frisbee and pushing strollers. Ducks quacked at the kids tossing bread into the water from a stone peninsula that jutted out into the middle of the lake. I inhaled the fresh crisp air and smiled. "I love this time of year where it's not too cold and it's not too hot."

He nodded. "Me, too."

We walked along the gravel path dodging kids running after balls and the occasional duck that had waddled onto the land. Once we were out on the trail away from all the people, I said, "So, any special reason you wanted to go for a walk?"

"No. It's just a nice day."

It gave me a warm fuzzy he wanted to spend time with me. It's not like Jane or anyone was here to witness his behavior. That helped counteract the disturbing news my mom had given me this morning. "My mom spoke to Gavin. He's stopping by tomorrow evening."

"That should be interesting."

I snorted. "Not the word I'd choose, but yes. I'm trying not to think about it. If I have a mental breakdown, can I come over to see—" I almost said *you*, but changed my mind and went with, "Ford?"

"Sure," he said. "Ford is always available for counseling."

"Thanks." I noticed he was carrying a bag.

"Did you bring bread for us to throw to the ducks?" I couldn't figure out what else he would have brought.

"Close." He pointed to a picnic table that was off the trail. "Let's sit over there."

I followed him and sat down on one side of the picnic table. He sat next to me and opened the bag. "You have your choice of roast beef or pastrami." He pulled out two, foot-long sub sandwiches and two bottles of water.

He'd brought lunch. How sweet. "I'll take half of the roast beef," I said. "You can have the rest."

"I'm up to the challenge."

We unwrapped the sandwiches and ate while we made small talk and watched other people who were also enjoying the weather. It was nice and comfortable. Sometimes being with him was so easy. Why couldn't it always be like this?

Chapter Twenty-Two

Matt

Monday morning at school I was nervous for Lisa. Knowing that the sperm donor was going to drop by had to be messing with her head. It was messing with my head, and it wasn't even my family drama. What did that guy think would happen? Anyone who'd done what he did should be contemplating wearing a bulletproof vest.

Lisa stood in front of her locker, furiously writing in a notebook. That was not the norm. She always had her homework done and probably double checked the day before it was due.

"What are you working on?" I asked.

She froze for a second and then continued scribbling. "Last night, I was so pissed about that jerk coming over I forgot to write an essay which is due today."

For about two seconds I considered making a joke about her grade point average being strong enough to handle it, but if I said that while she was upset she might try to stab me with her pencil.

"You'll finish it," I said instead, trying to offer moral support.

She snorted. "Yes, but the straight-A student in me is appalled that I let that idiot possibly affect my grade point average."

Not much I could say to that. "I'll be on standby after you meet with him tonight, in case you need someone to talk to, or a dog to hug."

"It's always good to have an escape plan," she muttered.

"You could avoid the whole situation and hide out at my house," I offered.

"Thank you." She sighed. "Honestly, I want to get it over with. I'm running scenarios through my head of all the reasons he could give for abandoning my mom and me. Nothing justifies what he did. I hate that I'm wasting time worrying about what he might say. I have better things to do with my brain cells." She scribbled a few more lines. "And done." She closed the notebook and stuck it back in her locker.

When she turned to face me, she looked so sad and stressed that I reached out to hug her before I realized what I was doing. She seemed startled, but then she leaned into me. It felt right. She fit perfectly in my arms, like she belonged there. And that was kind of terrifying. I tried to lighten the moment. "I could find out where he lives and deliver a truck full of manure to his front door."

"Eww." She stepped back from the embrace, but she was smiling. "Do you work with manure?"

"Not often, but I know where to order it and I could send it anonymously."

"Depending on how big of a jerk he is, I might take you up on that."

When I walked Lisa to her homeroom, I kept my arm around her shoulders. She didn't seem to mind. *What in the hell am I doing?*

The school day flew by. Lisa acted normal whenever I saw her, but she didn't have her usual spark. When I walked her out to the parking lot after school, she seemed distracted. I had to grab her hand to keep her from walking behind a car that was backing out.

"You don't want to die in a high school parking lot," I said.

"Sorry about that."

I knew what the problem was. "What time is he coming over?"

"After dinner, I think. When my mom told me, I kind of freaked out so I didn't hear all the details."

Once the car had moved on, I checked to make sure all was clear before we continued walking. "Want me to follow you home?" If I couldn't hit the guy, I could at least give her moral support.

"No, but thank you." She took a deep breath and let it out. "I'm telling myself it's not a big deal. I can handle this. Apparently, I'm a terrible liar because I don't believe either of those things."

"I'll give Ford a Minty so he'll have fresh breath for your therapy session."

"Thanks." She took her keys out but she didn't get into her car. Instead, she looked up at me with vulnerability shining in her eyes. "Can I have a hug?"

I opened my arms and pulled her in close. I couldn't think of a thing to say that would make the situation any better, so I just held on, trying to project reassurance and calm. The desire to protect her rose up inside of me. I inhaled and a lemony scent invaded my senses. It was nice, fresh and clean and no nonsense, kind of like Lisa.

She took a few deep breaths and then she looked up and met my gaze. Despite what I'd told her about not wanting my first kiss with a girl I liked to take place in a crappy parking lot, I focused on her lips. They sparkled in the light with some sort of makeup like it was a beacon attracting my attention. It would be so easy to lean down...close that distance between us, and brush my mouth across—

"I better go," she said.

I blinked and released her. *What in the hell am I thinking?* She didn't want me to kiss her. She just wanted comfort because she was afraid of what might happen when she met her jackass of a dad. *What kind of jerk am I?* I couldn't comfort her without thinking about kissing her? It's not like she wanted to kiss me. I needed to remember that. She didn't want me. She wanted Trey. And I didn't want her. I didn't. *Liar*...my brain screamed.

"Good luck." I hoped the confusion I felt didn't show on my face.

Lisa climbed into her car and then drove out of the parking lot. The sound of tires on gravel came from all around me. Like everyone else knew what they were doing, who they were with, and what they wanted. Sometimes it felt like I was striking out at all three.

Chapter Twenty-Three

Lisa

This wasn't a big deal. That's what I said over and over again as I drove home. It's not like Gavin was going to move in with us or request joint custody. He probably just wanted to say hello or something. Or maybe he was settling up accounts in his life because he was about to die. Not that I wished death upon him. Not really...okay maybe a little bit, because he was a miserable excuse for a human being, but not knowing why he was suddenly interested in my mom and me was making me a nervous wreck.

When I turned the corner, there was the white Honda parked in front of our house. What was going on? Gavin shouldn't be here already. He wasn't supposed to come until after dinner. Could the idiot not tell time? More than likely he had no respect for anyone else's schedule.

A slow burn started in my stomach. I parked my car and sat there, taking deep breaths, trying to get my emotions under control. I would not freak out in front of him. I didn't want him to have that kind of power over me. I wouldn't give him that power. Deep breaths.

Inhale.

Exhale.

Inhale.

Exhale.

Okay. I could do this. I checked my appearance in my visor mirror. Not that I needed his approval but I didn't want to look disheveled in front of him. Okay. Enough stalling. I exited the vehicle and headed up the walk.

When I put my key in the front door, my mom opened it like she'd been waiting for me. Instead of letting me come in, she came out onto the front steps.

"I'm sure you noticed the car. Gavin called. He asked if he could come early because he's going out of town on business." I could tell by my mom's pinched expression that she wasn't super happy about this, either. "Honey, if you don't

103

want to meet him, you don't have to. I'll tell him you're not ready yet. I'll ask him to leave."

Knowing she'd send him away made me feel better.

A black Impala pulled into our driveway. It was Tony, my mom's boyfriend. He climbed out with a worried expression on his face.

"If he's really obnoxious, can we have Tony punch him?" I asked, only sort of joking.

"No." My mom was using her therapist voice. "That wouldn't be appropriate, but you can say anything you want to Gavin."

"Really? Anything?"

She nodded. "This may be your only shot, so go ahead and get whatever you want to off your chest."

"Any language restrictions I should be aware of?"

Because if ever there was a situation that called for curse words, this was it.

"You can have some leeway," my mom said.

Game on.

I pushed past her and walked into the living room. Gavin sat on the edge of the couch like he planned to flee. "Getting ready to run away again?" I asked.

He sighed and sat farther back on the couch. "I deserve that."

"You deserve much worse than that."

My mom and Tony came in. Introductions were made.

Severe awkwardness ensued.

"I'm sure you have questions," Gavin said.

"You're right. I do. What type of dirtbag leaves his pregnant wife because he isn't ready to be a father?"

Gavin frowned. "I have no explanation except I was young and stupid. I know there is no excuse that will make up for what I did, but I wanted to apologize to you and your mother."

"Why?" I asked. "Why now? Are you in some type of assholes anonymous twelve-step program?"

"You have your mother's way with words." Gavin smiled.

"Well, it's not like I had a chance to learn anything from you."

"True. I'm here because after all this time I wanted to try to set things right, in some small way. I don't expect anything from either of you. I wanted the chance to meet you, Lisa, and to maybe help with your choices for college."

"How could you help with that?" I asked. Gavin looked at my mom.

She sighed. "I'm not saying we'll accept, but Gavin has offered to help pay for your college."

"You think any amount of money could make up for what you did?"

"No," Gavin said. "But it's the only gesture I can think of that might help both you and your mother."

Something about this wasn't adding up. "Why do you suddenly give a crap about us?"

"That's a fair question." He leaned forward. "And the truth will make you hate me even more, but here it is. I remarried a few years ago. My wife is pregnant. There's no way I can be a good father to my son while I know how badly I failed both of you."

A wave of anger washed over me, knocking me back a step. I didn't think it was possible to hate him more than I already did. I was wrong.

The temperature in the room seemed to spike or maybe that was the newfound hatred burning inside of me. No reason to hold it inside when I could spew it all over Gavin. "You are a complete piece of shit. You're not here because you want to make amends or because you want to get to know me. You're here because you want to ease your conscience."

He pressed his lips together like he was trying to figure out if he should say something more or keep it to himself.

"Speak your piece," I said. "It's not like I could think any less of you."

"I don't expect a miracle, but I hope in time that we can get to know one another."

"Don't. Hold. Your. Breath." I turned to my mom. "I've heard enough and there's nothing more I want to say, so I'm going to Matt's house. If you need help hiding a body later tonight, Matt's dad is a landscaper, and I'm sure he'd lend us his backhoe."

"Good to know." She hugged me and kissed my forehead. "Drive careful." She turned to Gavin. "Now it's my turn."

I almost wanted to stay and listen, but if I became any angrier I was afraid my head might actually burst into flames. I stalked out the door and dialed Matt on my cell.

"Hello?"

"Mental breakdown round two is in full swing. I'll be there in ten minutes."

"We'll be waiting on the porch."

When I pulled up to Matt's house, he was sitting on the porch swing with Ford and Chevy lying at his feet. I parked on the side of the driveway, got out, slammed my car door, and stomped up the stairs.

"I'm guessing it didn't go well," Matt said.

How to explain. "I've never been so pissed off in my life," I practically screamed. I told Matt about the fabulous reunion I'd had with my father, including the request to use the backhoe and then threw myself down on the porch swing beside him.

"Holy shit." Matt shook his head. "By the way, I can drive the backhoe, so we won't have to involve my dad."

"Excellent." It felt like anger was pulsing through my veins. "I hate him. And I don't mean I hate him like you hate someone you're mad at. I hate him like he's a cancerous blood-sucking leech."

"I hate him, too," Matt said, "if that helps. Man, I can't imagine what your mom is saying to him."

"I'm glad Tony is there with her."

Matt gave a low chuckle. "I think there's a zero percent chance that guy is leaving your house without getting punched."

I leaned into him, and he wrapped his arm around my shoulders. "I hope you're right. I'm normally a peaceful person, I don't like feeling this way, but I don't know how to make the anger go away."

Ford whined, stood up, and came close enough to put his head on my lap. He gave a low wag of his tail and looked at me nervously. I rubbed his velvety ears. "Such a sweet dog." He looked at me like I was the best person on the planet. Between Matt's arm around my shoulders and the furry therapist, my anger started to fade away.

"I think I need a dog," I said.

"Everyone needs a dog," Matt said. "Preferably two.

They're pack animals."

As I looked into Ford's big brown eyes and listened to him snuffle, I no longer felt homicidal. There must be something to animal therapy.

"Do you think your mom will accept his offer to help with college?" Matt asked.

"I don't know. I kind of hate the idea of taking anything from him. We've always lived on a budget. There's never been a lot of extra money. I can't imagine how my mom made it work when he first left her. So if taking the money makes her life easier now, then I'd agree to it."

"Shouldn't he have paid your mom some kind of child support after the divorce?" Matt asked.

"Huh, I never thought about that. I think he ghosted her, so she probably never had a chance to ask for help."

"Are you sure I can't punch him?" Matt asked.

"If anyone gets to punch him, it's my mom." I ran my fingers over Ford's head. His fur was soft and warm. "You should come live with me," I told Ford.

"No way," Matt said. "There are lots of dogs at the shelter who need a home."

"Maybe I could get a dog."

Chapter Twenty-Four

Matt

My dad came walking up to the front porch with dirt on his coveralls. He smiled at us. "You must be Lisa."

She nodded. "You must be Mr. Patterson. Do you mind if I steal Ford?"

He laughed. "It's nice to meet you, Lisa, but Ford is family. Haley can fix you up with a dog."

"That's what Matt said." She rubbed Ford's ears. "Guess I'll have to visit him here."

"Watch out, son. Ford's about to steal your girl."

Lisa laughed. I forced a laugh while silently wishing my dad would shut up. Was he trying to push me in what he considered the right direction? Or was he pointing out the obvious?

"I better go in and get cleaned up for dinner. Nice to meet you, Lisa."

"You, too." Once he'd gone inside, she said, "Your dad is nice. You're one of the few people I know whose parents are happily married."

"West's parents are married," I reminded her.

"Happily?" Lisa asked. "Because no one at that party seemed happy."

"They are awkward as hell," I said. "But they're happy." I studied Lisa as she rubbed Ford's ears. Her dark hair was kind of a mess but she looked beautiful. Why hadn't I seen her as datable when we first met? If I had, life would be so much easier.

"Matt?"

"What?" And Lisa was looking right at me. "Sorry, lost in thought."

"About?"

Nope. Not going to talk about it. "I was thinking about what kind of dog you should get."

"Something small and huggable would be best," she said.

"Probably." I kept staring at Lisa. I knew I was being way too obvious. Part of me hoped she'd realize what I was thinking. Maybe we could just slide into a real relationship. It seemed like the next natural move.

"Why are you looking at me like that?"

A car pulled up the drive, which kept me from having to answer that loaded question. It was Haley. Ford and Chevy trotted off to greet her.

"I feel abandoned," Lisa said as the dogs danced around my sister.

"Don't take it personally," I told her. "Haley is the dog whisperer. Plus she's the one who brought them home."

Haley stopped to pet the dogs and then came up the steps smiling at us. "Hey, guys." She looked at Matt and cleared her throat. "Aren't you going to introduce us?"

"Seriously?" Matt said. "You know who she is."

"Manners, Matt," Haley said in a mocking tone.

He rolled his eyes. "Fine. Haley, this is Lisa. Lisa, this is my pain-in-the-ass little sister, Haley."

Lisa grinned. "Nice to meet you."

"You, too," Haley said. "Jane will be pulling up any minute, so be prepared for another round of introductions." She went inside and the dogs followed her.

"Don't worry, she'll give them each a treat, and then they'll come back out," I said.

"What about Jane?" Lisa asked.

"I don't think she wants a Minty."

She snorted. "No. I mean Jane is going to see us being all couple-y. Should we act a certain way?"

Just like that, I was done. I had my arm around a smart girl who made me laugh. Why was I looking for someone else? "I'm not sure I care about that anymore."

Lisa tilted her head and looked at me like she didn't understand. The sound of tires on gravel meant Jane was about to make her appearance. She parked and bounded up the stairs. "Hello Matt and Matt's new girlfriend, Lisa."

Lisa laughed and responded, "Hello, Matt's sister
Haley's best friend, Jane."

"I like her," Jane said and then went into the house.

"Want to go somewhere with less traffic?" I asked.

"Sure." She sounded a little defensive. "Now that Jane has seen us."

"That's not what I meant. Charlie and my mom will come up the drive soon, so if we want some privacy we should relocate." I stood. "Let's go for a walk."

"Okay." She seemed a little uncertain but we stood and she let me hold her hand. We headed down the path that led to the greenhouses. Some of the flowers should be in bloom, and there were benches we could sit on out of the line of sight of anyone coming and going from the house.

The smell of soil and herbs filled the air. I loved that smell.

"What smells so good?" Lisa asked.

"My mom is setting up some herb garden planters." I pointed at the small troughs filled with rosemary, thyme, and basil.

"Smells like Italian food," Lisa said.

We walked over to a planting bench that was cleared off. Lisa sat, while I paced, trying to figure out the best way to break the news to her. Finally I gave up and went with, "I don't want to do this anymore."

"What?" Lisa's tone was hurt and angry.

"Wait. That came out wrong." I sat beside her and grabbed her hands to keep her from either hitting me or running away. "I mean, I don't want to fake this relationship anymore."

She wasn't saying anything, but she wasn't trying to flee the scene, either. I took that as a positive. I knew what I wanted to do. It was now or never. Moving slowly, I leaned in and brushed my lips across hers. When she didn't shove me off the bench, I pressed my mouth against hers again and slid my hand up her arm to the nape of her neck.

I felt her hesitate, like she wasn't sure what to do, and then she kissed me back. Her hands went to my shoulders and then slid around my neck. Everything seemed right in the world, and then she pulled away from me.

"Wait." She was slightly out of breath. "Why... What are you doing?"

I thought that was obvious. "It's you," I said. "I don't want Jane anymore. I want you."

"Why now? Is it because you feel sorry for me?"

"What? No. That's not it."

She scooted backward on the bench, putting some distance between us. "This isn't fair. I've had one hell of an emotional day and I came to you as a friend."

And now *I* didn't understand. This was supposed to be a good thing. "It's not like I'm trying to take advantage of you."

Her eyes narrowed. "I didn't say that. But the timing is odd. I liked you when we first met. You knew I liked you and you didn't even consider the possibility of dating me. It was straight to the friend zone."

She wasn't wrong. What could I say? "I didn't know you then, like I know you now."

"Guess what, Einstein, if you'd taken the time to get to know me instead of banishing me to the friend zone, we'd both be a lot happier right now."

"My bad," I said. "Listen, I wasn't looking to date anyone when we met because I had a crush on Jane. Now I see my crush on her has played out. I don't want her anymore. I want you." That had to count for something.

"If I wasn't Nina's friend who you were forced to hang around with all the time, would you have asked me out?"

That didn't make any sense. "If I didn't know you, how could I ask you out?"

She glared at me. "If you'd seen me at school would you have asked me out?"

How could I answer that? "If I say yes, you'll call me a liar. If I say no, you'll call me a jerk."

She blinked her eyes like she was trying not to cry. "Never mind." She stood to go.

"Wait. Please." I needed to find a way to make this right. "If we'd met and talked and you made me laugh, and we weren't thrown together because of our best friends, then yes, I would have asked you out."

Chapter Twenty-Five

Lisa

I wanted to believe Matt, but I didn't. I'd been around him for months and we'd laughed together and had fun and he'd never once seen me as datable. "I think you realized the Jane crush is going nowhere, and you feel sorry for me, and I'm convenient."

He stared at me like I was speaking a foreign language. "Convenient? You're not convenient. Do I feel sorry for you? Of course I do. Your douchebag of a sperm donor dad just dropped an emotional bomb on you. Me kissing you doesn't have anything to do with either of those things. I kissed you because I realized *you* are the person I wanted to be with."

"Maybe that's true. But did you ever stop to consider I might not want to be with you?"

He opened his mouth and then he stopped. "Fine. I'm

an egomaniac because I thought you'd want to kiss me back. You did. Didn't you?"

The way he said it, he wasn't asking for an admission of guilt. He looked completely confused. I kind of was, too. Trey had been talking to me and flirting with me and I was pretty sure if Matt and I broke up, Trey would ask me out. But, I still had lingering warm fuzzies for Matt. It wasn't fair for him to spring this on me. "I just can't...I can't deal with this today. Let's go back to our original plan. We pretend- date for two more weeks and then we see where we want to go."

That should give me time to figure out what I wanted to do.

"So you want to pretend the kiss never happened?" Matt was starting to sound annoyed.

"Yes." But I wasn't sure. I'd wanted Matt forever, but lately my mind had been focused on Trey. Trey hadn't friend-zoned me the moment he met me. He'd flirted with me. That had to mean something. "I think that would be for the best." And with the way Matt was looking at me, I needed to get out of there before I caved and kissed him again. Get away somewhere so I could think and figure out what the hell I wanted. "I should go."

Matt reached for my hand. "Wait. Kiss me goodbye. Kiss me and then tell me you just want to be friends. We can go back to the original game plan."

"Why would I kiss you goodbye?" Did he think I'd be overcome with lust? Right now I was more overcome with annoyance.

"I think you like me, too, and you're too stubborn to admit it. So kiss me goodbye and then we'll go back to fake dating."

This plan did not seem wise because I kind of wanted to kiss him again.

"Fine." The words slipped out of my mouth and a few seconds later Matt's mouth moved against mine. His hands wrapped around my waist, pulling me closer. And then rational thought fled the building as his teeth grazed my bottom lip. It seemed natural to tilt my head to the right as our lips parted and the world vanished. I gripped his shoulders tighter. I didn't want this to end. And then Matt's mouth moved away from mine. Cold air rushed into the warmth that had been building between us. I blinked back to the present, trying to figure out what was going on. That was it? He was just done?

I focused on his face. He was smiling at me. It was a know-it-all smile, more like a smirk, like he knew I wanted to kiss him again. This entire situation was his fault. I was not going to cave because he changed his mind. I took a deep breath and said, "Well, that was fun. I'll see you tomorrow." And then I stood and headed for my car, forcing myself not to look back.

Part of my brain screamed at me that I could have what I'd wanted before this stupid fake-dating situation. Another part of my brain said if Matt really wanted to be with me... and not because I was convenient, then maybe he should put a little effort into it.

On the drive home, I started laughing for no good reason except my life was a mess. I was pretty sure that was a sign of insanity. When I pulled up to the house, Tony's car was still there. Good. I'm glad my mom wasn't alone after dealing with Gavin.

I let myself in the front door and smelled pizza. My mom and Tony were curled up on the couch watching one of those *Matrix* movies they both loved.

My mom started to sit up. I held out my hand to show she should stop. "I'm fine. Are you okay?"

She smiled at Tony. "I'm happy." He beamed at her.

"Good. I'm grabbing some pizza and then I'm going to read in my room."

Once I was secluded in my room with two slices of meatball pizza and a bottle of water, I texted Nina to call me.

My cell rang before I could set it down on the bed. "How'd it go with your dad?" she asked.

I gave her a brief summary of my dad's piss-poor reason for wanting to meet me and his offer of cash.

"Take the son of a bitch for all he's worth," Nina advised.

"I might, but that's not even the headline of the evening."

I told her about Matt kissing me. She didn't respond right away. "What?" I snapped.

"Don't get mad, or madder, but isn't this what you wanted?"

"Yes and no," I said. "Just because he isn't interested in Jane, why does that mean I should automatically drop my crush on Trey?"

"I get it. Matt shouldn't expect you to jump on him just because he's suddenly interested."

"Exactly. Plus he looked a bit too sure of himself after he kissed me."

"Well, then I guess you wait and see how the next two weeks play out."

"That's the plan. Is it wrong that I feel like Matt deserves a little grief for being so slow on the uptake?"

"No. You don't want to be at his beck and call."

"Right."

"Hold on. West just knocked on the back door."

"I'm going to read and eat pizza, so you don't have to stay on the line with me."

"Text if you need anything," she said.

I sat on my bed eating pizza and reading an ebook on my phone. One of the things I liked about ebooks was how easy it was to read and eat at the same time. Flipping the pages required a mere tap of the finger which took much less coordination than holding a book open one-handed and turning the pages.

As I read, my mind drifted. What was I going to do about Matt? What did I want? Was it wrong that I was annoyed at him? Was I only annoyed because I was upset with the sperm donor?

The biggest question of the evening: should I drop the Trey crush and start a real relationship with Matt?

Chapter Twenty-Six

Matt

I sat on the bench and watched Lisa walk away from me. The sound of her car engine starting and tires crunching on gravel signaled she was driving away. What in the hell had just happened?

She liked me. I was sure of it. Was this all about timing? I'd blown her off when we first met. Was she going to hold that over me? It's not like I'd been mean about it. I'd treated her like a friend. That didn't make me a jerk. Clueless, yes, but not a jerk. Now what?

I headed into the house. Charlie sat on the couch, flipping channels on the TV. "I took your advice about Lisa," I said as I joined him on the couch.

"What advice?"

"You told me to choose her. I did. And now she's mad at me."

"What did you do?" Charlie asked. I summarized my epic fail.

Charlie rubbed his chin. "Yeah, that could have gone better."

"You think?" I grabbed the remote from him and flipped to an old episode of *Supernatural*. "Not sure what I should do now."

"Not much you can do except hope Trey isn't interested."

"I don't know what Lisa sees in that guy."

"Maybe it's his magical hair," Charlie deadpanned.

"Yeah, that's it. What really bugs me is I don't think he'd be into her if he knew how nerdy she was."

"Maybe you should help him find out," Charlie suggested.

"I'll keep that in mind as a last resort."

•••

Tuesday morning I went to school early and waited for Lisa in the parking lot. I wanted to talk to her with as few witnesses as possible. And I wanted to see her before she had a chance to talk to Trey.

Too bad I didn't have a clue what to say. When she pulled in and parked, I met her as she climbed out of her car.

"Good morning," I said.

"Morning." She looked at me like she was waiting for me to say something more.

"So this isn't awkward at all," I joked.

She smiled, which made me feel a little more confident. "About yesterday," I said.

"We're not doing this," she interrupted.

Umm...okay. "We're not doing what?"

"Doing this." She pointed back and forth between us. "We're not going to talk about what happened. We're going to pretend it never happened and move forward."

I reached up to rub the back of my neck. "Living in denial? Seriously? That's the plan?"

"Yes." She hitched her backpack higher on her shoulder. "We're going to go back to our regularly scheduled program."

"Remind me what that was again?"

"We pretend to date for the next two weeks and then let the chips fall where they may."

Not how I wanted to play this, but I could make it work for now. "Okay." I shrugged like it didn't really bother me. "If that's what you want."

She crossed her arms over her chest and gave me the once-over. "I thought you'd put up more of a fight."

"I would, I mean I want to, but I don't think that would help my case. So...I'll spend the rest of our time together showing you why I'm the guy you date."

"That sounds like fun." She walked past me and headed toward the sidewalk. I caught up with her and fell into step beside her.

"Do you work tonight?" I asked.

"No. You?"

"No. We should do something."

"Like what?" she asked.

"Whatever you want. We could go to the bookstore."

She snorted. "Wow. You must be serious about this."

"I'm even prepared to watch the rest of the Harry Potter movies."

She stopped walking and turned to me, throwing her arms out wide. "Why? Why now?"

I'd ticked her off. That much was clear. "Honestly. At first your nerdiness seemed kind of strange, but now I think it's cute."

"That's what every girl wants to hear." She shook her head and walked faster toward the door.

Well...that hadn't gone as planned, either. What should my next move be? I guess I'd figure this out as I went along and hope for the best. Lisa wasn't at her locker when I made it inside, but Nina and West were. There was a one hundred percent chance Nina knew every detail of what happened last night. Maybe she could give me some advice.

I approached Nina. "Remember when you told me to pick a lane?"

She nodded.

"Well I've picked one, but apparently I'm not doing a great job. Any suggestions?"

"Well," Nina said. "Your timing sucks, but I still think you can redeem yourself."

"How?"

"Show Lisa that you really know her and understand her," she said.

How was I supposed to do that? "So I should give her a bouquet of Harry Potter socks?"

Nina laughed. "That might be a good start."

The bell rang and I walked to class. Where had Lisa ended up? I guess I'd have to wait until lunch to try and make more headway.

At lunch, Lisa sat down and looked at me. "Remember our deal."

"The deal where we pretend for the next two weeks or the deal where I show you that I'm the better choice?"

"The first one," she said. "I never agreed to the second one."

"It doesn't really require you to agree."

She shook her head and muttered something I couldn't hear. I leaned in closer. "What was that?"

"I said, your timing sucks."

She wanted to argue about my timing? "Okay, Miss Overachiever." I opened one of my notebooks and drew an

X. "Here is where we met at Bixby's when Nina was stalking West."

"I wasn't stalking him," Nina argued. "We happened to be in the same place at the same time."

"Right. Anyway." I drew a line along the length of the page which ended at another X. "If you divide this into a timeline, we've only known each other a little while." I penciled in the day we'd met and then circled the rest of the line. "It's been a little over two months, so it's not like I ignored you for years and then suddenly noticed you."

She pointed at the piss-poor graph I'd drawn. "That first night we met at Bixby's I gave you a ride home. We laughed and talked and had a good time. Why didn't you think I was datable back then?"

"I was focused on someone else at the time so I wasn't seeing any girl as datable...any girl I met in that timeframe would have been friend-zoned. It wasn't just you."

"Oh," Nina sighed. "You were doing good up until that point."

"How is saying that wrong?" I asked.

"Because," Lisa said. "You lumped me in with every other girl on the planet. You didn't see anything special about me."

"That's some weird girl logic." I pointed at West. "Help me out here."

He glanced at Nina. She raised her eyebrows at him. "I plead the fifth," he said.

"Nice." I couldn't believe he was wussing out on me. I tapped the timeline. "This proves I didn't ignore you. I needed to get to know you. Maybe you saw the possibility of a relationship when we first met and I didn't because I was preoccupied. That doesn't make me a jerk."

"No," Lisa said. "It doesn't. But it also doesn't make me feel like I was your first choice."

I opened my mouth and then closed it. What could I say? She wasn't my first choice. My first choice had been Jane. I couldn't change that. I pointed at West. "It took a while for him and Nina to get together. That doesn't mean he didn't think she was special."

"He's not wrong," West said. Nina nodded in agreement.

"See, they agree with me."

"Let's not argue about this," Lisa said. "The whole point is that we work our way through two more weeks so we can figure out what we want."

"Wrong. I figured out what, or who, I want. Now it's your turn to do the same."

"Fair enough," Lisa said.

"Don't forget we're stuffing book baskets for the library after school," Nina said. "Matt, you and West are welcome to join us."

"No thanks," West said.

I looked at Lisa. "I could help if you want."

She shook her head. "No thanks. I think I need some girl time."

I glanced at Nina and then back at Lisa. "Why does it feel like you're going to be plotting against me?"

"Not plotting," Lisa said. "Just dissecting every single thing you've ever said and trying to decipher your true motives."

"Great. Have fun with that."

Chapter Twenty-Seven

Lisa

"Are you just tormenting Matt, or do you not know what you want?" Nina asked as we sat at my kitchen table that evening, putting together the book baskets for the library fundraiser.

"That's a good question. I'm not sure I have an answer at this time." I tied a blue ribbon around the handle of a basket. It came out crooked, so I untied it and started over. It came out much better the second time.

Nina ripped open another bag of Easter grass. "Okay, let's change the question. If you'd never met Trey, would you agree to go on a date with Matt?"

I laced another ribbon through the braided handle of the basket to dress it up a bit. "Yes, but I have met Trey so that question is invalid."

"I'm trying to be the voice of reason here, but you aren't making it easy." She stuffed the basket with grass and then nestled two gently used books inside it along with a bag of jelly beans, some Peeps still in their wrapper, and a couple of bookmarks I'd crocheted. "Here's another way to look at it. Matt is a sure thing. You know he's into you."

"I know." I tied a purple ribbon on a new basket and added matching purple grass. "Part of my brain is telling me to kiss Matt and forget about Trey, but another part is pointing out that Trey flirted with me the first time we met while Matt banished me to the friend zone without giving me a chance. That kind of ticks me off."

"Guys are weird," Nina said. "It's not like West realized he was into me right away." She laughed. "The first time we talked he told me I was one of the strangest people he'd ever met."

"And you continued talking to him?"

"Yep." She added some notebooks, pens, candy, and a book to the purple basket and then set it in a clear Rubbermaid storage container along with the others we'd finished. While the baskets wouldn't win any prizes for presentation, they should bring in a few dollars for the library.

"So the moral of the story is I shouldn't judge him too harshly for not seeing me as datable until he knew me better?" Because that still didn't sit well with me.

"I don't think there is a moral to this story except that teenage boys are a little slow when it comes to relationships." Her cell buzzed. She checked it and grinned. "Speaking of relationships, I'm meeting West for dinner. Do you want to come with us?"

"No thanks. It's Taco Tuesday so Mom and I are making Mexican tonight."

"Cool. I'll see you tomorrow." Nina carried the clear plastic bin of Easter book baskets out to her car. I cleaned up the stray bits of fake grass that seemed to have some magnetic level of static electricity. Every time I thought I'd found the last piece another one appeared, stuck to the table leg or my shoe.

I checked the clock on the microwave. My mom would be home in about half an hour. I put the meat on the stove and then grabbed the lettuce and tomatoes. There was something therapeutic about chopping lettuce into ribbons. Slicing the tomatoes wasn't nearly as much fun. I added the taco seasoning to the meat, and my mouth watered at the spicy smell.

My mom came in just as I was taking the meat off the stove.

"Happy Taco Tuesday," I said.

She inhaled. "That smells wonderful."

We filled our plates and then took our food outside onto the patio. I bit into my taco and the shell split down the middle, breaking into several pieces. "And now it's Nacho Tuesday."

My mom nodded with her mouth full. After swallowing, she said, "That doesn't have the same ring to it." She added a little more salsa to her taco. "So what's new with Matt?"

"Why do you ask?" What kind of mom radar did she have going on?

"Just curious to see how it's going."

"It's going." I didn't want to rehash my social life. Guys weren't the only thing I was concerned with. "Nina and I made some book baskets for the library fundraiser."

"Is that why there's a purple plastic string stuck to the bottom of your glass?"

I checked and sure enough, there was a piece of Easter grass on the bottom of my iced tea. "This stuff is like the glitter of the Easter world. It sticks to everything and you never know where you'll find it."

She grinned. "You should have gone with the edible candy grass."

"We talked about it, but that would've stuck to the books."

"And the plastic grass won't?"

"Yes, but the plastic stuff won't ruin the books."

"True."

"Plus the candy grass tastes weird."

"I don't know," she said. "I liked the green apple kind."

Wait a minute. "I don't ever remember any green apple-flavored grass in my Easter baskets."

"It never made it that far." My mom grinned.

•••

Wednesday morning, I smacked my cell when the alarm went off. Why did I feel so groggy? I rubbed my eyes. I'd had such a bizarre dream. Something about an amusement park. I was riding a roller coaster. It was one of those giant beasts with loops and hills and a tunnel. Half the time Matt was in the car with me. The other half of the time Trey was. When we did a giant loop, the lap bar came undone and I fell out. Matt grabbed my arm at the last second and kept me from falling hundreds of feet. I was so relieved, but then he let go and hollered, "You should have known better than to trust me," as I fell to what probably would have been my death, except I woke up at that point.

Thank you, brain, for a stressful night's sleep. After breakfast I felt a little more with it, but I couldn't get the dream out of my head. What was my subconscious trying to tell me?

At my locker, I found Matt waiting for me. He held what looked like a brick. Why was he holding a brick?

"Morning," I said.

"Good morning. I wanted to ask your opinion on something." He held out the brick.

Now I could see he'd painted one side of it to look like the spine of an old leather-bound book. "That's pretty cool."

"Thanks. Do you think I should try to put titles on them?"

"Depends. What are you going to use them for?"

"I thought they'd be fun to use in someone's landscaping."

"If we had a library, you could use them there," I said.

"Or a bookstore," he said. "Maybe I'll make up a few different kinds and post them on our website. If people see them and like them, they can place a special order." He leaned in and said, "I could make you a Harry Potter set."

It was a nerdily romantic gesture. "I'd like that."

"Good." He put the brick in his locker and then he turned around and grabbed my hand, pulling me closer until we were toe to toe.

Butterflies flitted around in my chest. "What are you doing?"

"Playing my part." He leaned down and brushed his lips across mine.

The contact was brief, but my lips tingled and I felt myself smiling at him like a lovesick idiot. "Smooth move," I said.

"I thought so." The bell rang and he walked me to homeroom, holding my hand the whole way. And damn it if it didn't feel right.

Chapter Twenty-Eight

Matt

It felt like I'd finally managed to do something right. Lisa liked the Harry Potter book-bricks idea. She wasn't mad at me for kissing her in school. That had been a risk. She could have pushed me away, but she didn't. The timing had been perfect, since Trey had been walking toward us. That's not the only reason I kissed her but it was a bonus. It might have been a little sneaky. Too bad. I planned to play up our fake relationship in public. Having Trey see us happy together might convince him to pay attention to another girl so Lisa could stop thinking about him. And it's not like I'd only be doing it to put on a show for Trey. I'd act how I'd normally act in public, if Lisa really was my girlfriend. Then, eventually she would be.

The day flew by. When I walked Lisa to her car after school, I was feeling pretty good about the whole situation.

"Do you work tonight?" I asked her as she leaned back against her car.

"No. You?"

"I have some work to do before dinner," I said, "but I'm free after. We could walk the trail at the park."

"Sounds good."

I leaned in and she moved away from me. "I thought you said if you liked a girl you wouldn't want to kiss her in a crappy parking lot." She smiled as she said it, so I was pretty sure she was teasing me.

"That was for a first kiss." I leaned in and said, "We already had our first kiss, so now parking lots are fair game."

"Oh, I guess I missed that lesson in the how to date like a normal girl class."

"That's the wrong class," I said. "You'd be assigned to the cute nerd-girl class. No normal girls allowed."

"Is it wrong that I take that as a compliment?" she asked.

I snaked my arm around her waist and pulled her close. Instead of answering, I kissed her. She didn't seem to mind. The noise of the parking lot drifted away.

...

At dinner, Haley said, "So things seem to be going good between you and Lisa."

My parents and Charlie all stopped talking and focused on me.

"Thanks for making me the center of attention," I said.

"I know how you love that." She grinned.

Charlie laughed.

"Jerk," I muttered.

"Ignore them and tell me about your new girlfriend," my mom said. "I think everyone has met her except for me." Sometimes my mom had her feelings hurt over weird things, so I said, "She was gone by the time you came home the other night. I'll make sure to introduce you the next time she comes over."

"What's she like?" my mom asked.

"She's cute, and smart, and she loves Harry Potter."

"What do her parents do?" my dad asked.

"Her mom is a relationship counselor." I didn't feel right telling anyone about the sperm donor.

"And her dad?" my mom prompted.

"Not in the picture."

"That's sad," my mom said.

"I don't think it bothers her." Time to deflect. "The herb planters are looking good."

"Thank you. I think they'll be perfect for people who want to grow fresh herbs in their kitchen windows."

The rest of dinner went fairly smooth. After we were done, I headed out the front door and down the path between the greenhouses. When I was far enough away that I knew Haley wouldn't be eavesdropping, I called Lisa on my cell. The call went to voicemail. I hung up and texted her since no one I knew ever checked their voicemail.

Something bumped my leg. I looked down to see a small blond shaggy dog with sad eyes. Had Haley brought another foster dog home from the shelter?

I squatted down. "Hey buddy, where'd you come from?" I reached out to pet his head and he tried to crawl into my lap. "It's okay." I picked him up and held him. He leaned into me and whined. "Don't worry. You came to the right place."

He couldn't weigh more than fifteen pounds. I could feel a collar on his neck but I couldn't see it through his fur. Hopefully, he had tags. I carried him back to the house and inside to the kitchen. Charlie was the only one in the vicinity. He looked up from the couch and came to join me. "Where'd your new furry friend come from?"

"He was out by the greenhouses." I sat at the kitchen table and checked his collar. No tags, but someone had wrapped a piece of notebook paper around the fabric of the collar and stapled the paper shut.

"Open that," I told Charlie.

He tore the paper off the collar and unfolded it. *Harry is a good dog. My parents won't let me keep him. I know Haley works with dogs. Can you please find him a new home?*

"Harry?" I said.

The dog's ears perked up. "I think that's his name," Charlie said.

"Someone who knew Haley dropped him off here? Why not take him to the shelter?"

"People are weird," Charlie said.

My dad came into the kitchen and looked at us. "Did Haley bring home another dog?"

"No." I told him about the note.

"Didn't your girlfriend say she wanted a dog?" My dad came over and rubbed Harry's head. "You said she likes Harry Potter. Seems like fate to me."

"Not a bad idea." My phone buzzed with a text. I checked the message. Lisa was done with dinner. I texted back that I was coming over and I was bringing her a surprise.

"Be sure and take some dog food with you," my dad said. "One less reason for her mom to say no."

Charlie grabbed a Ziploc bag and filled it with dry food. Then he offered a handful to Harry. The dog sniffed and then chowed down.

"Maybe you should have been named Hoover," I said. Harry barked and wagged his tail. "Come on. Let's go."

"Wait a minute." My dad went to the junk drawer and pulled out a red ribbon, which he tied to Harry's collar. He twisted the ribbon around and shaped it into a bow. "Presentation is important."

On the ride to Lisa's house, Harry lay on the passenger side floor whining. "I swear I'm not dropping you off somewhere. If Lisa can't keep you, you can come home with me."

When I parked at Lisa's, he stood up and gave a low wag of his tail. "Come here," I said.

He hopped onto the seat and I picked him up. I knocked on the front door and hoped Lisa's mom wouldn't be the one to open it. Thankfully, Lisa greeted me. Her eyes went wide. "You brought me a dog?"

I entered the house and headed over to the couch. I sat and settled Harry on my lap. Lisa sat next to me. "Harry, this cute nerd-girl is Lisa. I think she might be your new owner."

Lisa held her hand out so Harry could sniff her. "Hey, puppy."

He gave her hand the once-over and then licked her palm. That was a good sign. She ran her fingers over his head. "He's so cute. Where did he come from?"

I relayed the story of the note. "He seems like a good dog."

"That's so sad someone had to give him up. It's not like he's a big dog."

"He kind of fits the small person theme you have going on around here," I teased.

"Yes, he does. Come here, petite puppy." She picked him up and moved him to her lap. He froze for a second like he wasn't quite sure what was going on.

"Poor little guy." Lisa held him and rubbed his ears. "It's okay." He relaxed and leaned into the caress.

Lisa's mom came into the living room and tilted her head as she studied the situation. "Matt, did you give my daughter a dog?"

"Maybe?" I couldn't tell if she was mad or confused. "I mean, if you guys don't want him, I'll keep him. So no pressure."

"Mom?" Lisa said. Harry whined.

Best not to start off this relationship with Harry peeing on the carpet. "We should probably take him outside."

Lisa stood and I followed her into the kitchen and out the back patio doors. She set Harry down. He trotted over to the grass, hiked his leg, and then came right back over to us.

"I think he's potty trained," I said.

"Who's a good dog?" Lisa said. Harry did a small happy wiggle, glanced around panting, and then went back up to the patio doors and pawed at the glass.

"I think that's dog for, *Please don't leave me out here by myself*," I told her.

"No worries, Harry." Lisa opened the door and he went back into the kitchen and started sniffing around.

"He probably needs a bowl of water."

"I can fix that, but I don't have any dog food."

"I brought you some, but I left it in the truck in case your mom objected."

Lisa grabbed a bowl and filled it with water. She glanced around the kitchen and then placed it next to the cabinet. "Here you go."

Harry lapped up some water, splashing it on the floor. "You might want to put a tray under the bowl," Lisa's mom said from the doorway to the living room.

Lisa grabbed what looked like cookie sheet from one of the cabinets. "This will work until I can buy him something better."

Chapter Twenty-Nine

Lisa

I couldn't believe Matt brought me a dog. It was such a sweet thing to do. I know the dog just showed up at his house and he could have taken it to the shelter, but the fact that he thought to bring him to me gave me a warm fuzzy. "Is his name really Harry?" I asked. "Or are you hoping my Harry Potter obsession will convince me to keep him?"

"Total coincidence. I can show you the note," Matt said. "It's still at my house."

It seemed like fate.

Harry finished drinking and then came over to sit down in front of me. He tilted his head like he was asking a question. It was instinct to bend down and pick him up. He snuggled against me and then he glanced up at me like he wasn't sure if he should. "It's okay." I held him a little tighter and he relaxed. I could feel his heart beating. This must be why people fell in love with small animals. They needed you and they made you feel loved.

I carried him back into the living room and sat on the couch. He wiggled off my lap and turned in a circle next to me before lying down and putting his head on my thigh. He exhaled and closed his eyes. His warm head on my leg gave me a feeling of contentment. "He's so cute." I looked at my mom. "Can we keep him?"

"I'm not sure," she said. "We know nothing about taking care of a dog."

"All you need is food, water, and a dog bed." Matt sounded like the voice of reason. "Maybe some toys and chewies."

"Where will he stay while you're at school and I'm at work?"

Good question. "Matt, what do you suggest?"

"You could baby gate him into the kitchen. That way if he has an accident it won't be hard to clean up."

"We don't have a baby gate," I said. "But we could block the door with a couple of laundry baskets or chairs."

"Matt, will you take Lisa shopping and show her what she needs to buy to keep Harry happy and healthy?"

Matt nodded. "I brought food in my truck. We could take him to PetSmart with us right now, but I think his former owner dumped him off tonight. Another car ride might freak him out."

"How could anyone drop him off?" I rubbed Harry's ears. His fur was a lot thicker than Chevy's or Ford's but it was just as soft.

"At least they didn't dump him on a street." Matt reached over and ran his hand down Harry's back.

No matter how irritating he could be sometimes, Matt was a good person who cared about furry creatures. That was a huge plus. I don't think I could be with someone who wasn't kind to animals.

"Do you want me to run out to the truck for his food?" Matt asked.

"That's probably a good idea so we don't accidentally forget."

Matt stood and walked to the door. Harry's head popped up. He turned his head, looked at the door, and whined.

"He's coming back," I said.

A few moments later, Matt opened the door and came back in. Harry's tail fluttered back and forth and he gave a small bark.

"I'm not sure if he's happy to see me or the food," Matt said. "Probably both."

"Do you think he's hungry?"

"He had a handful before we came over. Dogs his size only need a cup of food for the whole day. You could give it to him all at once, but at my house we always break it up into two or three meals because when you eat he'll want to eat, too."

Matt walked into the kitchen and set the bag of food on the table before coming back to the couch. "I was going to ask if you wanted to go for a walk but I'm thinking that's not an option now."

"That's okay. We can just stay here and bond with Harry."

"I'm glad you like him."

"Me, too." While I enjoyed snuggling with Harry, I had the sudden desire to be in closer proximity to Matt. "Since you're here, do you want to watch the next Harry Potter movie?"

"Sure."

I picked Harry up and we headed to the kitchen, through the pantry, and down the stairs into the basement. Harry sniffed the air like he wasn't quite sure what to think about this new development.

I sat down next to Matt and set Harry on my other side. Once the movie was up and running, Matt put his arm around my shoulders. I smiled at him. "Classic move."

"Thanks." He looked quite pleased with himself. "I read about it in the How to date like a normal guy handbook."

"I'm guessing that's the companion book to How to date like a normal girl."

"It is." He pulled me a little closer. "I'm still working on the next chapter, How to convince the girl you like that you belong together."

"Any good tips in there?"

"Just the basics. Give her a dog, then lure her into the basement to watch Harry Potter so you can kiss her."

"That's oddly specific," I said.

"It's a magic book. You tell it your troubles and it adapts to your situation."

"Really?" I had to give him points for originality.

"Yes. Now, you're supposed to watch the movie. I'll lean in, being very smooth, and kiss you."

"Okay." I grinned and turned my eyes to the screen. "I'll just watch the movie and wait for you to bring on the romance. Do you need to stretch or anything first? I wouldn't want you to get a cramp."

He snorted. "I think I got this."

It took effort to keep my eyes on the movie, because I knew Matt was going to kiss me, and I wanted him to kiss me, but it still made me a little nervous. He seemed to be taking his time. I cleared my throat. "Any minute now."

"I was about to move in."

"Sure you were," I teased.

"Hey what's that?" Matt pointed to the side of the television.

Instinct made me turn my head to look. Matt leaned in at that exact moment and pressed his mouth against mine. Sneaky. I almost laughed, but then he wrapped his arms around me and pulled me close and it didn't seem funny anymore.

The world drifted away. He cupped the back of my head with one hand while the other slid down to my hip. Being with him like this, kissing him, felt exciting and intense, and a little bit scary, but a whole lot of right.

When the kiss ended, he leaned his forehead against mine. We were both breathing a little heavy. I had no idea what to say.

After Matt left, Harry followed me around like he was a baby duck. When it was time for bed that night, I wasn't sure where he would want to sleep. I didn't have a dog bed, so I put him on a pillow in a laundry basket next to my bed. He sat in the basket and looked at me in confusion.

"*Woof.*" He pawed at the side of the basket and then whined.

"That's your bed," I said.

He laid his head on the edge of the basket and stared at me, with soulful, sad brown eyes. So, of course, I caved. "Come here." I climbed out of bed, picked him up, and put him at the foot of the bed before climbing back under the covers. "Good night, pup."

He commando-crawled up to the top of the bed...slowly, like he didn't think I'd notice. He pawed at the covers and tried to shove his head underneath.

"You want under the covers?" What kind of weird dog behavior was this?

I lifted the blanket and he shimmied under and lay there. Maybe he was cold. I grabbed my cell off the nightstand charger and Googled dogs sleeping under covers.

Some small dogs like to burrow under the covers, creating a den-like place to sleep.

The article went on to say he'd find his way out if he became too hot. I worried he couldn't breathe under there, but apparently he wouldn't have a problem finding his way out.

Chapter Thirty

Matt

When I woke up Thursday morning, everything felt right in my world. Lisa's mom had let her keep Harry, which was great for two reasons. First off, Harry had a good home. Second, every time she looked at him, she'd be reminded of me. It made out-of-sight, out-of-mind a little harder for her to achieve. And I was good with that.

Whenever we were together things were great. Last night, in the basement...let's just say I'd developed a whole new appreciation for Harry Potter. Thinking about her made my heart beat faster. She was the one for me. She had to know that now...right?

When I got to school and met up with Lisa in front of her locker, she was yawning.

"Good morning."

She glared at me. "It's your fault I didn't get any sleep last night."

I'd left her house by nine. "What do you mean?"

"My new best friend wanted under the covers, and then on top of the covers, and then under the covers. It's a good thing he's cute."

"Maybe he was nervous since he's in a new home."

"Maybe." She yawned.

"Want to go to PetSmart after school? We can find him his own bed."

"I doubt he'll want to sleep in it, but I need to get him a bowl and some food, so that sounds like a plan."

"Cool."

She yawned again. "We may need to hit a Starbucks on the way there."

"We can do that." Out of the corner of my eye, I noticed Trey's stupid hair coming down the hall, so I put my arm around Lisa's shoulders. She didn't comment, she just smiled at me.

"I wonder if my teachers would mind if I napped through class," she asked.

"From personal experience, I've learned the only class you can sleep through is study hall. Even then, the teacher gets a little cranky."

The bell sounded for homeroom. I walked Lisa to her class. The rest of the day flew by without any Trey sightings. Hopefully, he'd taken the hint and given up.

After school, I followed Lisa back to her house to drop off her car and then I drove to Starbucks. "Do you want to drive through, or do you want to go in?" Normally, I hated going in, but girls seemed to like sitting in coffee shops, so I thought I'd let Lisa choose.

"I'm snacky," she said. "Let's go in."

"Snacky? Is that part of Lisa's Lexicon?"

"Yes," she said. "Along with hangry which I'm going to be if I don't eat soon, so delay me at your own risk."

"Inside it is." I parked in one of the last open spots. It would probably be crowded.

I opened the door into the coffee shop.

Lisa inhaled as she walked in. "I love the smell of fresh baked carbs and coffee."

"It's kind of crowded." There were people in line but not that many tables. Hopefully, they'd all be full and we could go back out to my truck.

"I can grab a table while you order," Lisa said.

Great. "Sure. What do you want?"

"A blueberry muffin or scone and a large coffee with cream."

"I can remember that." I stood in line, shuffling forward. When it was my turn to order, it took me a minute to realize Trey was the one taking my order. His hair was up in a baseball cap.

"Hey, Matt. What can I get you?"

I blinked. "Didn't recognize you without the hair."

"Sadly, they have a policy against cool hair."

"That's too bad." I grinned and then ordered.

"Coming right up." He made the coffee and grabbed the scones I ordered. It could have been awkward, but it wasn't. Like he was so sure of himself, he didn't mind talking to me. Which was impressive and annoying at the same time.

When he handed me my change he said, "Tell Lisa I said hello."

I nodded, even though there was no way I'd mention that I'd seen him. Unless she spotted him behind the counter, and then I'd pretend to remember because all is fair in love and war. I almost tripped over my own feet. Love? I wasn't in love with Lisa. I just liked her better than other girls. That wasn't necessarily love.

When I went to find the girl who I was not-in-love-with, I spotted her at a table for two. There was a guy at the table next to her leaning in and saying something to her. Whatever it was, he was ticking her off.

I approached from behind the guy so she could see me coming but he couldn't. I bumped his chair hard. He whipped around.

"My bad," I said.

The guy nodded and moved his chair closer to his friend. He leaned in and said something that made the other guy laugh.

I sat down and passed Lisa her coffee. "What's wrong?"

"Some people are idiots," she muttered before taking a drink of her coffee.

"Like that guy?" I asked. "What'd he say to you?"

Her cheeks turned red. "Nothing worth repeating. Let's just eat and go."

That didn't work for me. I turned around to the jerk at the next table. I recognized him from school. "Why does it feel like I should punch you?"

"I don't know," he said. "You'd think after keeping her up all night you'd be more relaxed." His friend laughed.

What was he talking about? And that's when I got it. This morning at her locker. Somehow her comment about not sleeping last night had hit the rumor mill and been taken the wrong way. "I gave her a dog. *He* kept her up all night."

"Seriously?" the guy said. "That's just sad."

"You're just an asshole." I really wanted to punch this guy, or at the very least shove him out of his chair. And I was about thirty seconds from doing that when Lisa put her hand on my arm.

"Let's leave," she pleaded.

I ground my teeth together in frustration. I looked at her. "I really want to punch him."

Her face was redder than it had been before. "Can we go?"

"Your call." I picked up my coffee and the bag with the scones and followed her to the exit.

Once we were in the truck, I said, "Are you okay?"

She nodded. "He said something stupid to embarrass me and it came out of nowhere and for the first time in my life I had no words."

I cracked my knuckled. "Still want to punch him.".

"That won't accomplish anything."

Wrong. "It would make me feel better."

She grabbed the bag with the scones. "Maybe after I eat I won't be so mad."

"I'll still be mad." I ate my scone and drank my coffee and tried to figure out what to do next.

Once she'd finished eating, she sighed. "Nope. I'm still fantasizing about having you punch him."

"I can do that," I said.

"No. My mom says sometimes you have to ignore the idiots of the world and move on with your own life. Let's go buy some toys for Harry."

"Okay." I could go along with that plan for now. Then I'd point the guy out to Charlie and he could accidentally elbow him in the face during gym. It was a good system. That way the guy would know it was from me, but Charlie could claim it was an accident and I had nothing to do with it. Justice would be served.

At PetSmart, Lisa perked back up. We walked up and down the aisles checking out dog toys, collars, and leashes.

Chapter Thirty-One

Lisa

"Can you go grab a cart?" I asked Matt.

"Sure." He headed up to the front of the store. I picked up a dog toy shaped like a bunny. Watching Harry chomp on a cute furry rabbit might be mildly disturbing, so I set it down and grabbed a stuffed toy shaped like a hot dog. Much less disturbing visual.

I was trying not to think about what that guy at the coffee shop had said to me. I'd never been the object of slut-shaming before and as far as I was concerned no guy had the right to talk to a girl like that...whether she'd slept with her boyfriend or not. It was none of his or anyone else's business.

Matt came toward me, pushing a cart. He stopped suddenly and seemed to be listening to someone off to his right. Then he turned the cart and headed in that direction.

What was going on? Had someone mistaken him for one of the employees? Maybe a little old lady was asking for help reaching the cat food on the top shelf. That was just the kind of thing Matt would do. I was thinking warm fuzzy thoughts about him when I peered around the corner and saw him talking to a certain blonde. A blonde he supposedly no longer cared about. I ducked back down the aisle and headed over to dog leashes and collars.

Why was he talking to Jane? He said he was over her. Wait. What was I thinking? He'd known her forever. I'm sure she practically thought of him as a brother. There was no reason for me to be concerned. Matt would probably tell me all about it when he brought me the cart. No need to worry.

I focused on picking out a cute leash and collar. "There you are." Matt came toward me with the cart.

"Took you a while," I said. "Did you run into someone you knew?"

"No." He picked something up out of the cart. "I was hunting down Minty's for small dogs."

And he'd just lied to my face. Why would he do that? There was only one reason to lie. He was still into Jane. I shouldn't jump to conclusions. I gave him another chance.

"I thought I heard you talking to someone."

He reached over and picked up a camo leash. "Oh, right. I bumped into Jane."

"And you weren't going to tell me because…" I hoped he'd fill in the blank with an answer that wouldn't tick me off.

"Because I was just saying hello to a friend and if it had been anyone but her I would have told you. I figured we'd had enough drama for the day."

"Don't lie to me again," I said. "Even if you think the truth will upset me. I have to know that I can trust you."

"You can, and I won't do it again."

"Okay." I grabbed a navy blue leash and collar set. "What kind of food should I get?"

"They make the same kind we buy Chevy and Ford in small dog size." He pushed the cart and I followed along beside him, feeling a little less good about this whole situation.

By the time we checked out, I just wanted to go home and hug my dog.

Matt helped me carry everything into the house. Harry did the puppy dance of happiness, spinning in a circle, and then he made a beeline for the back door.

"Right." I ran over and opened the door. He dashed out to the grass and did his business. "He really is a good dog. It's kind of sad that someone loved him but couldn't keep him."

"He has a good home now," Matt said. "And that's all that matters."

"Would you really have kept him if my mom said no?"

Matt nodded. "Absolutely. Since I can't keep him, I think I'll keep you instead."

"Oh, really?"

He reached out and pulled me close. Speaking in a quiet voice, with his mouth right next to my ear, he said, "You're cute, and small, and soft, and cuddly." His warm breath hit my neck and my ear, sending a shiver down my spine. "And I think you should be my girlfriend."

Rather than answering him, I turned my head and kissed him. Heat flowed between us, making it hard for me to think. *This one*, my hormones screamed. *We want this one.*

Harry barked, pulling me from the hormonal haze I'd fallen into. I blinked, looking around. Matt appeared as stunned as I was.

Harry scratched at the glass patio doors. "He must want food," Matt said.

I wasn't capable of rational thoughts at the moment, so I walked over and opened the door for Harry. We followed him inside where I opened the bag of dog food and put about ten pieces in his new bowl.

It took him three point five seconds to make the food disappear.

"Isn't he supposed to chew his food?" I said to Matt, since between us he was the dog expert.

"Yeah, but I don't think he knows that."

Harry walked over to the counter where I'd left the PetSmart shopping bag. "*Woof.*"

"I think he knows that stuff in the bag is for him," Matt said.

I walked over and pulled out the bag of long-lasting chew sticks. "You'll have to use your teeth on these." He sniffed the small twisted-up piece of rawhide I held out to him, chomped down on it, and trotted into the living room where he lay down under the end table.

"Now that he's taken care of..." Matt grabbed my hand and pulled me to the couch. He kissed me, and it seemed like the most natural thing in the world. Maybe this could work out. Maybe we did belong together.

•••

"I'm definitely experiencing the thank God it's Friday feeling today," my mom said as she sat across the kitchen table, drinking her coffee with her eyes half closed.

"Me, too," I said, because it's what she expected to hear. Truthfully, I wasn't sure. The days seemed to fly by. A week from tomorrow was our three-week deadline. Matt and I hadn't talked about that yesterday. If I didn't bring it up, he'd probably completely ignore it.

"How are things going with Matt?"

"Good... Confusing but good."

"Why confusing?"

"I don't know. I really like him. He's kind and protective and cute but he lied to me yesterday." I told her about running into Jane at the pet store.

"That's not a deal breaker," she said, "but I don't like it."

I felt the need to defend him, so I told her about the jerk at the coffee shop.

"Okay…Matt's definitely looking better. I've never understood why so many men have a Madonna Whore complex."

"What does that mean?"

"Women are either sacred virgins or streetwalkers. There's no in-between, which is ridiculous because women are people and sex is a normal part of a grown-up relationship. Some men still don't seem to get that. And while we're on the topic, you do know that you can talk to me about anything."

"Yes, but can we not talk about it right now? Please. You already explained the birds and the bees so I'm good."

"I'll just hit the high points. You're smart. Love can make you stupid. Never let any guy pressure you into doing anything you don't want to. Never believe the everyone else is doing it line. You're better off waiting until college or later. And always insist on a condom." She grinned.

"There. I think that's it."

"Thanks for that completely awkward breakfast conversation."

"You're welcome. Now you better go get in the shower."

Once I cleaned up, I surveyed my wardrobe options. Today felt like a comfortable T-shirt and jeans kind of day. The one good thing about dating Matt is he didn't care about what I wore. If I decided to date him…because we weren't really dating. Then again, we weren't really faking it anymore, either. He'd asked me to be his girlfriend yesterday. I hadn't answered him but I had kissed him. Did he think that meant he was my boyfriend? Why was this dating stuff so complicated? I swear I could feel a brain cramp coming on.

Whatever it was we were doing, he knew me already and had seen me with makeup and without and he didn't really distinguish between the two styles. That was a bonus. Some girls wore makeup all the time. That was their choice. If it made them happy then I didn't think people should comment on it. I preferred the more relaxed approach. I didn't feel like putting that much effort into my face for a normal school day so I went with my light pink lip gloss and a messy bun.

Chapter Thirty-Two

Matt

I woke up on Friday in a good mood. Lisa hadn't officially answered me when I asked her to be my girlfriend, but she hadn't said no, either. Things were moving in the right direction. I just couldn't mess up again like I had when I'd lied to her about talking to Jane. No more keeping the truth from her. Not that I made a habit of it, but little white lies seemed to be better than hurting someone's feelings. Especially if the truth wouldn't change anything.

After breakfast I checked the time on my cell. I could pick Lisa up for school if she wanted a ride. Would that be weird? West gave Nina a ride to school every day. As Lisa would say, it was a couple-y thing to do, so I called her.

"Hey," she said. "I was just about to get into my car. What's up?"

"That's why I'm calling. Do you want me to come get you? We could ride to school together."

"Oh..."

She hesitated a little too long. My neck muscles tensed up. "Never mind," I said. "I'll see you there."

"No. Wait. Nina and I were heading to the bookstore after school, so that will work. I just need to text my mom, so she doesn't wonder why my car is still here."

"Cool. I'll be there in a few minutes." And I could relax again.

I drove across town, wondering what West and I would do while Nina and Lisa did their book thing. We'd figure something out. Lisa was smiling when I picked her up.

"Good morning," I said.

"Morning." She climbed in and buckled up. "Do you know what today is?"

"Friday?" I hoped she wasn't going to bring up our deal because as far as I was concerned we weren't playing that game anymore.

145

"Well yes, but it's also buy a book from the clearance section and get one free day."

"Do we need to fix up your bookshelf so it can hold more weight?" I asked.

"Maybe." She grinned. "I like that you don't judge me for my book habit."

"As long as you don't expect me to read them, too, we're good."

"You know...Nina and West read together."

"I hope that's not a deal breaker," I said, "because it's not happening."

"That's okay. People need to have separate interests."

"We should meet up after the bookstore like before when you ran into us at The Slicery."

"That sounds good."

I hit every green light on the drive to school. I decided to take that as a good sign. The school parking lot was crowded, but I found a spot up front because someone was pulling out. Another good omen.

"You seem happier than usual today," Lisa said as we walked across the parking lot, holding hands.

"Things seem to be falling into place." I squeezed her hand but didn't say anything else at the risk of freaking her out.

When we reached the lockers, Nina and West were there like normal. Not so normal was the addition of my sister's best friend pacing in front of my locker with a worried expression on her face.

"Hey, Matt. I hoped I could talk to you before school," Jane said.

I dropped Lisa's hand and moved closer to Jane. "Is everything okay?"

"Yes. It's just that I have this plan and it's a good plan but no one else seems to agree." She reached out and grabbed my hand. "And I was hoping I could count on you."

"Sure." I liked that she thought she could count on me. "Whatever you need."

Someone cleared her throat behind me. I turned to see Lisa looking less than pleased.

Crap. I pulled my hand away from Jane's.

"Did I suddenly become invisible?" Lisa asked.

"What? No. I could tell Jane needed help with something."

"Sorry," Jane said. "Do you mind if I steal your boyfriend for a few minutes?"

"I might mind." Lisa crossed her arms over her chest. "What did you need to talk to him about and why don't you want me to hear it?"

"Oh." Jane blushed. "No, it's not that I didn't want you to know. I didn't really think about you...and now this is awkward, isn't it? Anyway, I want to throw a surprise party for Haley next weekend, and I need Matt's help to make it work. I can pay you in cupcakes."

I looked at Lisa. "Jane makes amazing cupcakes. Want to help me help Jane throw a party for my sister?"

"What's the party for?" Lisa asked.

"Her birthday is next month, but I know she'll be expecting a party then so I wanted to surprise her," Jane said, like that made total sense.

"So it's a surprise because it's not your birthday, surprise party?" Lisa said.

"Yes." Jane bounced.

"Please don't encourage her." Nathan, Jane's perfect boyfriend, came walking toward us.

"You don't know what I'm doing," Jane said.

"You bounced. It's a dead giveaway." Nathan came up and put his arm around her. "We discussed this. Bryce wants to throw her a surprise party."

"Yes," Jane said. "On her actual birthday. This one is early so it's not the same. Right?" She looked at me to back her up.

"*Umm*," Lisa said. "I'm not sure your logic makes sense."

I laughed. "It's Jane logic so in Jane's universe it makes perfect sense."

"Exactly," Jane said.

Lisa backed up a step. "So what you're saying is the universe revolves around Jane."

Shit. "No."

At the same time, Nathan said, "Yes."

Jane beamed at Nathan. "If that's true then shouldn't you agree to help me?"

"I walked right into that one, didn't I?" Nathan said. "Come on. You can tell me what you want to do and I'll pretend it's a great idea."

"Thank you." Jane bounced and then grinned at me. "See you guys later."

"See you," I said.

Once they were far enough away that they couldn't hear us, I turned to Lisa. "So, that was kind of funny."

"Not the word I'd use to describe it," she said.

"Oh come on, you can't be mad that she asked me to help her plan a party for my sister."

"Do you remember when we were walking down the hall holding hands, you were all happy about maybe being my boyfriend and then you spotted her and dropped my hand like it was covered in slime?"

"Okay...maybe that's how it felt but that's not how I meant it. I could tell she needed me."

"You practically glowed when she said that crap about knowing she could count on you."

"What's wrong with that? I'm happy she thinks I'm a dependable guy."

"Because that makes you seem more datable?" Lisa arched an eyebrow at me.

"No." How could I reel this situation back in?

"You know what? Maybe your universe does still revolve around her."

"No, it doesn't. Understanding her quirky logic doesn't mean I want to be with her."

"Please," Lisa said. "If she'd come to tell you that she'd broken things off with Nathan, you would have welcomed her with open arms."

"I appreciate the jealousy, but you don't have anything to worry about." How could she not understand?

"Jealous? You think I'm jealous?" Lisa grabbed my arm and dragged me toward a less crowded area of the hall. "I'm angry, you idiot. I'm angry because you lied. You said you wanted me. The only reason you want me is because she isn't available. I deserve better than that. I deserve someone who picks me as their first choice."

The bell sounded for homeroom and Lisa walked away muttering to herself. I stood there, trying to figure out how my life had gone to hell in the last fifteen minutes. Was I never supposed to talk to Jane again? That seemed unrealistic. She was my sister's best friend. She was around all the time.

The weird thing was I enjoyed talking to Jane because she was different. She didn't think like everyone else. On the way to first hour, I updated West on the situation. "What do you think?"

"You can't avoid Jane for the rest of your life to make Lisa happy. She needs to get over it."

"Any idea on how I can say that in a way that won't piss her off?"

"No." He clapped me on the arm. "Good luck with that."

"Thanks." I had until lunch to come up with what I wanted to say to Lisa. How could I fix this? I may have been a little too quick to rush to Jane's aid, but that didn't mean Lisa wasn't overreacting. But...I probably shouldn't lead with that.

Lisa sat at our lunch table staring at her phone. Did she plan to ignore me? I wasn't going anywhere so she'd have to talk to me eventually. I pulled out a chair and sat.

"If you think I'll go away because you're ignoring me, you're wrong."

"Stalk much?" she muttered.

"Funny." I took out my sandwich. "I see Jane as a friend. I see you as girlfriend material. Those are two different things."

"We're not doing this here." Lisa's voice broke, like she was trying not to cry.

Shit. I set my sandwich down and reached over to touch her hand. "I'm sorry this upset you. There's no reason to be upset."

"Do you feel inferior to Trey?" she asked out of nowhere.

"No. We're two different kinds of people."

"Jane and I are both funny and smart, but she's blonde and quirky and I could bleach my hair but I'll never do a cute little bounce thing when I'm excited. I'll never be as cool as Jane."

"You're cool in your own quirky nerd-girl way. You make me laugh. I like you. Why isn't that enough?"

Chapter Thirty-Three

Lisa

Maybe it should be, but it wasn't. My dad hadn't wanted me. And maybe that was the root of my insecurities. Who knew? But seeing Matt light up around Jane made me realize he didn't act that way around me.

"I deserve someone who looks at me the way you looked at her," I said.

Matt reached up to rub the bridge of his nose. "She might make me laugh, but I wouldn't watch Harry Potter movies for her."

"So you don't actually like Harry Potter? You were just pretending?"

He opened his mouth to speak and then stopped. After a deep breath he said, "I had a crush on Jane. You came along and made me forget about her. Even if she was single right now, I'd choose you. I don't want to kiss her. I want to kiss you."

His words were sweet, but they didn't ring true. "I call bullshit on that statement."

"Listen. Jane will always be around because she's my sister's best friend. I can't change that. I won't go out of my way to spend time with her, but I shouldn't have to apologize for talking to her."

His rational argument didn't change the way I felt. "How do I know you're not just waiting around for when she's available?"

"Did you see the way she and Nathan act around each other?" Matt said. "They aren't going to break up anytime soon. Even if they did, I'd choose you. That has to count for something. Right?"

Okay. He sounded sincere. Things had been going so well between us. I'd trusted Matt. Trusted that he'd always be there for me. And then he'd dropped my hand and rushed to her side.

"I need some time to think," I said.

Matt leaned back in his chair. "Here's something for you to think about. My crush on Jane is in the past tense. I chose you over her. You still have a thing for

Trey. I'm not freaking out about him because I trust you. Why don't you trust me?"

He wanted to throw Trey in my face? Fine. "You know what? I think this experiment has gone on long enough."

"You're still thinking of us as an experiment?" Now he sounded mad.

"Honestly, I don't know what we're doing anymore."

"I think it's called dating," he said. "At least that's how I saw it."

How I felt about Jane may not be rational, but I didn't know how to shut the emotions off. I'd never been into self pity. I dealt with life as it came along. For some reason, this was messing with my head. "Matt, I know I'm being weird about this. I just need a little time to think. Can you give me that?"

"Can you not be mad at me while you think?" He reached over and put his hand on my forearm.

I managed a small smile. "I will try."

"Can we still meet up for pizza after you buy out the bookstore tonight?"

I nodded.

"Am I crazy?" I asked Nina in the girls' locker room as we changed into our gym clothes.

"You'll have to be more specific," Nina said.

I stuck my tongue out at her. "About Matt. Am I overreacting because I'm insecure that I'll never live up to a certain standard?"

"You mean the standard of the person who isn't you, that he doesn't want to date?" Nina asked.

"Thanks for the sarcasm. Now knock it off and help me fix my brain."

"Fine. Matt may smile at another girl, but he's meeting you for pizza. I think that tells you all you need to know."

"Are you and Matt fighting?" Clarissa asked. She'd walked up behind me.

"Sort of," I said.

"Maybe you two were better off as friends," Clarissa said.

"Why do you say that?" I asked.

"You've been less happy," she said. "And I feel like a terrible person, and you can never mention this to Charlie, but if you and Matt broke up I know someone who might ask you out."

"Trey?" I couldn't believe this.

She nodded. "Should I not have told you?"

"It's better she knows," Nina said. "This way she has options."

Hello, irony. This was playing out how Nina had joked it might. I could pick who I wanted to be with. There was one problem. How did I know if I wanted to be with Trey unless I went on a date with him? How could I go on a date with him without hurting Matt's feelings?

The gym teacher blew his whistle so we hustled out into the gymnasium for roll call.

"Today we are starting our unit on square dancing," he announced with almost perverse glee.

"Shoot me now," I muttered to Nina.

Chapter Thirty-Four

Matt

After school, I waited at our lockers to meet Lisa so I could give her a ride home. I still wasn't sure where I stood with her. Right now I was grateful she'd agreed to keep our date tonight. I had a feeling in my gut something wasn't right. And I had no idea how to fix it.

When she came toward me down the hall, her smile was a little dim, but she looked better than she had at lunch. I'd wracked my brain trying to come up with something to show her she was the one. That I liked her and all of her nerdy, bookish ways.

She stopped walking mid-stride and turned around. Someone must have called her name. She backtracked and disappeared from view. Where'd she go? I headed toward her and spotted her talking to Trey. My first instinct was to storm over there. But I'd told her I trusted her. And I did, but I didn't trust him. Had he heard we were fighting and come to see if he could snake his way between us? I ground my teeth and stalked back to our lockers, pretending nothing was wrong.

When she came to meet me, her smile was gone. What did that mean?

"Hey," she said, not quite meeting my gaze. "I'm going to ride over to Nina's house with her and West."

"I can give you a ride." I did not like where this was going.

"No. I think Nina and I are going to stay in and have a girls' night."

"Why can't you look at me?"

She raised her gaze to mine. What was that in her eyes... guilt?

"Are you still my friend?" she asked.

A cold feeling settled in my stomach like I'd eaten a bag of ice. "I'd like to think I'm more than that."

"We made a deal as friends, that we'd date, and then break up."

And that's when I got it. "You want to break things off with me so you can date Trey."

"That doesn't make me a bad person," she said. "It's what we agreed on."

She was right. That was the deal, but I'd changed my mind. Now what? There had to be a way to save this.

I knew Trey wouldn't be into her Harry Potter nerd-girl themed life. How could I outsmart them both? "I remember agreeing to show you that I was the one you should date." Before she could argue, I said, "And our deal was supposed to last one more week."

"It was," she said.

"But you're just going to be counting down the days until you can go out with Trey," I said. "So why don't we change the deal? We don't have to be exclusive. I mean I won't be dating anyone else while you figure out what you want, but you can go on a date with Trey."

"You're being strangely reasonable about this," she said. "If you were doing this to me, I'd be pissed."

I laughed. "You have no idea how badly I want to track Trey down and break his nose, but I'm not going to do that because I know in the end you'll make the right choice. So I can deal with it for now. Are we still on for pizza tonight?"

"I guess so," she said.

"Okay." I could leave her to ride home with Nina but that might give Trey an opening to talk to her and I didn't want him getting any closer today. "Come on. I'll give you a ride to Nina's."

I didn't give her a chance to argue. I started walking and hoped she'd come with me. I wanted to hold her hand or put my arm around her shoulders but if Trey was watching it should look like things were a little off between us...like we might be breaking up. I needed him to get a false sense of self-confidence going so I could trip him up in the end.

After dropping Lisa off at Nina's, I drove home, trying to figure out the best way to handle this situation. Jane and Haley were seated in the kitchen when I walked in. The way they stopped talking made me suspicious.

"Were you talking about me?" I asked.

"Indirectly," Haley said. "We heard you and Lisa weren't getting along."

I could use their help in this little conspiracy, so maybe it was time for me to come clean. "Here's the deal. When Lisa and I were just friends, I told her that I used to have a crush on Jane."

"What?" Haley and Jane shouted in unison.

I could feel my face heating up. "I know it's weird. But it's in the past."

"Okay," Jane said.

"Thanks for sharing the awkward," Haley chimed in.

"I'm only telling you because this morning, Jane stopped to talk to me about something." I wasn't going to give Jane's party idea away. "And Lisa was there, and she got the crazy idea I was still interested in Jane."

"You're not...right?" Jane said.

"No. You are firmly in the sister category."

"Good," Jane said. Then her cheeks colored. "Not that you aren't a great guy but—"

"It's okay," I said.

"So I made Lisa jealous?" Jane said. "But she saw me with Nathan."

"I know, but she thinks you're cool and she calls herself a nerd-girl and I think you intimidate her."

"I could talk to her," Jane offered.

"Not a good idea," Haley said. "Coming from someone who has had their share of insecurities, your self-assured blondness would just make it worse."

"Oh," said Jane.

"You guys might be able to help in another way." I sat down at the table with them. "Instead of breaking up, I told her we didn't have to be exclusive. I know Trey likes her and he's probably going to ask her out."

"Clarissa's cousin?" Haley said. "Does Clarissa know?"

"That is not a road I want to go down. I don't want to mess up Charlie's relationship. I kind of want Trey to ask her out so she can see that she should be with me, not him."

"That could backfire," Haley said.

I glared at her. "That's the point. I need to come up with something to show Lisa I like her nerdy side. I don't care that she isn't cool. I like that she's into books."

"There's lots of Harry Potter stuff out there," Haley said.

Exactly what I'd been thinking. "Lisa and Nina are going to the bookstore tonight. I know they have Harry Potter bags there. Can you go by and pick one up for me?"

Haley pulled out her cell phone. "Let's check out the bookstore website so we can see what they have."

Ten minutes later, I had picked out and purchased a book bag, a Hermione pen shaped like a wand, a Gryffindor notebook, and several pairs of Harry Potter socks which would be ready for pickup in the store in half an hour.

"She wears Harry Potter socks?" Jane said like she was slightly horrified by the idea.

"Yes." I grinned. "She does."

"Do you wear Harry Potter socks?" Jane asked.

I laughed. "No. I don't."

"Would you wear them if you had them?" Haley asked. "I could pick up a pair for you."

"No thanks," I said. "Just stick to the plan."

"That's not nearly as much fun, but okay." Haley stood and stretched. "We can run and pick your stuff up now."

"Thanks."

Chapter Thirty-Five

Lisa

I sat in Nina's kitchen nursing a cup of hot cocoa while we dissected everything Matt had said.

"Doesn't it seem like he gave in too easy?" I asked.

"Well, I think he really does like you as a friend and as a girlfriend and he's trying to do the right thing," Nina said.

I frowned into my cocoa.

"What? You wanted him to argue with you?" Nina said. "Because you can't have it both ways. Either he gives you room to see what you really want, or he argues and tries to change your mind."

I watched the marshmallows melt in the brown liquid. "I guess he's kind of doing both, isn't he? He insists he is the right guy for me but he's willing to let me figure that out for myself."

"So he's being a good friend," Nina said. "Which is really mature, or suspicious. He must really believe you and Trey won't hit it off."

"He thinks Trey won't be into my nerdy side," I said.

"If he doesn't like Harry Potter, he's out," Nina said. "Best friends don't let best friends date anti-Potter people." My cell dinged with a text. I glanced at it, assuming it was my mom or Matt. It was Trey. Crap. I hadn't expected to hear from him so quickly. I'd told him Matt and I were going through a rough patch and he'd said to let him know when I was available.

His text said, "Are you free Saturday night?"

I showed the text to Nina. "Now what?"

"It's your decision. You could go out with him next weekend."

"I won't stop thinking about it until I know." I texted back. "Maybe. What's up?"

He sent me a link to a band playing at a local restaurant. "Music and food?" I showed Nina. "What do you think?"

"It could be fun."

I texted back. "Okay."

"Are you still with Matt?"

I texted back. "Not exclusive.:

"It's a start."

I turned my phone off. "Why do I feel guilty?"

"Because Trey and Matt are both good guys," Nina said.

"But it's not like you're lying to anyone. Everyone knows what's going on. You might not even like Trey."

"I'm ready to hit the bookstore," I said. "Maybe I'll buy myself that Harry Potter bag so I'll feel better."

"Retail therapy is always a fun idea."

When we reached the bookstore, the Harry Potter bag I'd liked was gone. A few of the others were cute, but none of them really worked for me. I went up to the woman behind the checkout counter. "Do you have any more of those Harry Potter mailbags?"

She pulled something up on her computer screen. "Sorry. Someone bought the last one about five minutes ago. I could send for one from another store."

"No thanks."

"You could order it online," Nina said as I stood there pouting.

"No. If I was meant to have it, it would still be here."

"Now you have more money to spend on books," she added.

"I guess that's a good way to look at it." The giant buy one get one free sign over the clearance section called out to me. I could always count on books to make me feel better. The staff must have rearranged the sections because where I normally found paranormal young adult, I was

confronted with self-help books.

How to Tell if He's the One was next to *Dating for Dummies*. I pointed at the books. "It feels like the universe is mocking me."

Nina grabbed my hand and dragged me over to the young adult section. "That's not the universe. It's the bookstore manager's way to get you to look at books you might not normally buy."

Forty-five minutes later, I was the proud owner of four new books. The world seemed like a brighter place. My bookworm high lasted until we walked out to Nina's car and then my palms started to sweat.

"What am I going to say to Matt?" No matter how fair this supposedly was, I felt like a jerk.

"Whatever you'd normally say to him. Nothing between you guys has to change."

I snorted and looked out the window.

"Seriously," Nina said. "He agreed to seeing other people. Everything is above board here. Just act like you would on a normal date."

"Normal is not my area of expertise," I muttered.

Matt and West already had a table at The Slicery.

"Find any good books?" Matt asked when I sat next to him.

He was acting normal. Good. Maybe this wouldn't be so weird. "I found four."

"Are you planning on picking up an extra bookshelf on the way home tonight?" he asked.

"That's not a bad idea." The waitress came and took our order. Matt and I split a meatball pizza. Nina and West went with sausage and mushroom.

"I've never understood mushrooms on pizza," I said. "They feel like erasers when you bite into them."

"Have you bitten into a lot of erasers?" Matt asked.

"A few," I admitted. "I used to chew on my pencils in grade school. Once we switched to using pens, I stopped."

"Speaking of pens," Matt said. "I saw something and it made me think of you." He pulled a small brown paper bag from his jacket pocket and passed it to me.

"What's this?" I asked.

"Just something to show that I know and like the real you," Matt said.

The brown paper crinkled as I opened the bag and pulled out a pen shaped like Hermione's wand. "I love it." I opened the package and tested the pen on the paper bag. The ink was a vibrant blue. What a sweet thing for Matt to do. I smiled at him. "Thank you."

"You're welcome. I'm glad it gets the nerd-girl seal of approval."

"Suck up," West said from his side of the table. Nina poked him in the ribs. "I think it's cool." "Technically, it's the opposite of cool," West said.

"Says he who has read all of the books," I shot back.

"There's a difference between reading them and collecting fan merchandise," West said.

Nina rolled her eyes. "Who did I catch looking at the Hogwarts Lego castle online?"

"I wasn't looking for myself," West objected.

"Right," I said. "You thought Matt might like it for Christmas."

"Oh, look. Here comes the pizza," West said.

The waitress delivered our food so I let the topic drop. It was funny that Nina and I both reveled in our bookish nerdiness, while West was more of a closet nerd. Matt didn't fall into the nerd category, but he didn't judge me for my nerd-girl ways and he thought what I did was cute. And I know he bought me the Harry Potter themed pen to make a point, but in the end it was a valid point, so it wasn't that sneaky. The idea of going on a date with Trey started to seem less appealing.

At the end of the night, Matt gave me a ride home. He parked his truck in front of my house and an awkward silence descended.

"Do you want to come in and see Harry?" I asked because I couldn't think of anything else to say.

"I don't think so." Matt leaned toward me and I met him halfway. His lips barely touched mine and then he pulled away. "Good night."

That was it? Okay. I looked at him. Earlier tonight he'd seemed genuinely happy. Now his expression seemed a little bit tight and brittle. Maybe he was thinking about me kissing Trey. I didn't know what to say, so I went with, "Good night."

...

Saturday morning, my mom woke me up with the words, "Bacon, maple syrup, and pancakes will be ready in five minutes."

Sitting up, I inhaled the savory scent of bacon combined with the sweet scent of maple syrup. "Oh, that smells like heaven."

I joined her in the kitchen, poured myself a glass of milk, and then dug into the yumminess waiting for me on the kitchen table.

"*Woof.*" Harry pawed at my foot under the table.

"I don't think you can have bacon," I said. "But I'll feed you." I grabbed a handful of brown pebbles from his food bag and tossed it in his bowl. He sucked the food down before I made it back to my seat.

"*Woof.*"

I looked at him and then at my mom. "Are we giving him people food?"

"I don't think it's good for him," she said.

"Pancakes aren't really good for us, either," I pointed out. "I mean, they feed your soul but aren't fabulous for your calorie count."

"*Woof.*" Harry chimed in like he agreed.

My mom sat down opposite of me and broke off a tiny piece of bacon. Harry did a furry tap dance as she lowered it down to him. When it was a foot from his mouth, he jumped and grabbed it from her hand like a tiny furry piranha.

"Wow. He's serious about his food." Harry turned his gaze on me. "One more piece," I said. I broke off a corner of my bacon strip and dropped it from the edge of the table. He jumped and caught it midair.

Despite Harry's intense staring, we managed to eat the rest of our breakfast without giving him any more food.

"So what are you doing tonight?" my mom asked.

I'd already told her about Matt saying we could see other people. "I'm going to hear a band with Trey."

"And why do you say that with the same enthusiasm as talking about having a cavity filled?"

I poured more syrup on my pancakes. "Guilt. I like Matt a lot, but I feel like I should get the chance to see how things could be with Trey."

"And Matt is giving you that chance."

"Hence the guilt," I said.

"No matter how old you are, relationships are tricky," she said. "I would give you the when it's right you'll know it speech, but my life didn't work out that way."

"You thought Gavin was the one?"

"He was at the time. Now, when I look back, I realize he was self-centered, selfish, and immature. At the time, I thought we were perfect for each other."

"And now you love Tony."

"I do," she said. "But if I'd met him when I was twenty it wouldn't have worked. When you get older you see who people are rather than the image they project to the world."

"So find someone who likes you for who you are instead of who you pretend to be?"

"Sort of," she said. "It's probably best if you just be who you are instead of pretending to be someone else, but that's hard to do. We all have our public personas. I wear Wonder Woman pj's at home, but I couldn't dress that way at work and inspire confidence in my clients."

I grinned. "I don't know. Some of your clients might think it was fun."

"You know Matt likes who you really are. Find out who Trey is and see if you can be yourself around him. If you can't then that should help you make your decision."

For my date with Trey I tried to pick an outfit that was me, but on a slightly cooler level. It was kind of like wanting to make a good first impression for a job interview. I wasn't going to be fake but I wasn't going to break out my full nerd-girl until I'd tested the waters.

A black sweater with blue jeans and black Keds seemed like a good choice. My Harry Potter socks beckoned from my sock drawer. I usually wore them with my Keds. The black ones with owls and Harry Potter glasses on them were fairly subtle and they made me smile.

When Trey picked me up, he looked ultra-cool in ripped jeans, his leather jacket, and a plain white shirt. And of course his hair was awesome. He smiled at me from the doorway, like he was happy with what he saw, too. That was nice.

"Come on in." I stepped back so he could come inside and do the obligatory meet the parent maneuver.

My mom stood in the doorway to the kitchen holding Harry. Apparently, Harry didn't agree with my assessment of Trey because he was growling.

"Trey, this is my mom and that ferocious beast is Harry."

"Nice to meet you," Trey said to my mom.

"Nice to meet you, too. Have fun tonight."

"Bye, Mom." When we left my house, Harry started barking. "Sorry about the dog."

"That's weird," he said. "Most dogs like me."

"Do you have a dog?" I asked.

"No. We have three cats. They think they own the house." He turned on the radio and a punk rock song blared through the speakers. He must have seen me flinch, because he toned down the volume. "Too loud?"

"Just a bit," I said.

"I like to feel the music," he said. "My dad tells me unless it rattles your bones it's not loud enough."

I laughed. "Interesting way to look at it." I hoped the band wouldn't be painfully loud or this was going to be a very long night.

"The Crazy Eights are pretty loud, but they're playing on the outdoor patio so it should be okay. I was happy to see a band I recognized down here. I was afraid the music scene would be pretty bleak."

I knew zero about the music scene. "My mom and Tony like to listen to acoustic guitar. Unplugged bands play at the mini-amphitheater in the park every summer. I've gone to a couple of those concerts."

We made small talk, and I was pretty comfortable with Trey. He obviously wanted to be with me. No one had forced him to hang around. He'd chosen me, and that made me feel special, though I wasn't sure we had much in common.

The restaurant was kind of artistic in its own way. The inside walls were mostly exposed brick. The tabletops had been painted in different colors and patterns. Paintings and drawings hung on the walls like they were on display at a gallery. Once we were seated, I noticed that the chairs were mismatched and so were the plates and silverware.

"This place is pretty cool."

"I heard about it in art class. The art teacher's dad owns it. Sometimes he displays student work." He pointed at the paintings on the far wall.

"Are any of those yours?"

"I wish," he said. "There's a waiting list to have your work displayed and some people have been on it for months. My name won't reach the top until after I graduate."

"Is that what you want to do?" I asked. "Paint?"

"I love to paint, but I'm not sure it would pay the bills. I think it would be cool to open a place like this. In Chicago there are some restaurants where the chefs make food that looks like art. What about you? What do you want to be when you grow up?"

"I'd like to be an author, but like you said, I'm not sure it would pay the bills. I could see myself being a librarian or managing a bookstore."

The waitress came and took our order. I chose an eclectic salad that came in a blown glass bowl. Trey ordered a burger. I was starting to relax when the band plugged in for their sound check. The blast through the speakers made me jump.

Trey laughed. "You might be a little high strung."

"I startle easily." I was glad the band was outside and we were inside, because otherwise it would have been painfully loud. Even at this level it was difficult to make conversation. So I ate my salad and smiled.

When we finished our food, Trey said, "Let's go out on the patio."

Great. Just what I wanted to do...go closer to the loud noise. I nodded and followed after him. He found us a couple of seats on the corner of the patio, and while the band was okay the volume was so loud it rattled my teeth. Everyone else on the patio seemed to be into it, so I smiled and tapped my foot to the beat.

When they took an intermission, Trey said, "Aren't they great?"

"They're good." I excused myself and went to the restroom where I texted Nina. "Trey is nice. Band is too freaking loud."

She responded. "Put little balls of Kleenex in your ears to cut the sound."

Huh. Okay. I gave it a shot, rolling little pieces of tissue and sticking them in my ears. The noise around me dropped a bit. Hopefully, it would help with the band. I pulled the impromptu earplugs out and put them in my pocket before going back to Trey.

He wasn't at the table where I'd left him. I had a moment of panic until I spotted him talking to the guitar player who had similarly cool hair but it was streaked black and red. When he came back over he was grinning.

"Do you know him?" I asked.

"He was a senior when I was a freshman. I knew who he was, so I introduced myself."

"That's very extroverted of you," I said.

"I'm not shy." He reached across the table and slid his hand around mine. "How about you?"

"If you gave me a choice of talking to ten people I'd never met or locking myself in a room for twenty-four hours with a stack of books, I'd choose the books."

"Really?" He seemed surprised. "I thought anyone who yelled their thoughts to the universe on a Monday morning would be more outgoing."

"I don't keep my opinion to myself very well," I said. "But I'm not chatty."

"Interesting combination." The band started up again so we stopped talking. Trey held my hand so I could only slip the ball of rolled-up tissue into my left ear. At least I'd be able to hear out of one ear tomorrow.

Deciding to go with the flow, I listened to the music and people-watched, and had a decent time. When the band stopped playing half an hour later, I prayed they weren't just going on another break.

Trey frowned. "That was a short set." He released my hand. "I'll be back in a minute."

"Okay." I pulled out my cell and checked the time. The band had played for an hour. It hadn't seemed like a short set to me.

When Trey came back he had a flyer in his hand. "I didn't want to leave without grabbing the band's list of upcoming gigs." He folded the paper and put it in his pocket. "Are you ready or did you want dessert?"

"I'm good." I didn't want to order dessert because what if the band decided to do an encore? I'd reached my limit on loud noise for the evening.

When I scooted forward in the seat, my pants leg came up exposing my socks. Trey looked at them in confusion. "Are those owls on your socks?"

I nodded. "Owls and glasses."

"Okay. Why are there owls and glasses on your socks?"

"I thought they were cute," I said.

"Must be a girl thing." He grinned. "Guys don't do cute socks." He took his keys out of his pocket without commenting further. "Let's go."

We walked together out to the parking lot. Was his comment on the socks positive, negative, or neutral? It was hard to tell.

On the drive home, the closer we came to my house, the more nervous I became. Would Trey kiss me? It was a first date. I'd been on a few of those and not all of them had ended in a kiss. Being the extroverted guy he was, I assumed a kiss was imminent. Did I want to kiss him? I wasn't sure.

When he pulled up in front of my house he said, "Sorry if the band wasn't really your thing."

"I liked them." I did. "I'm just not a loud noise person."

"I hope you had fun anyway." He reached over and held my hand.

"I did."

"Cool." He leaned over and pressed his mouth against mine. It was awkward for a few seconds and then not so awkward.

When I pulled away, he was smiling at me. "Maybe we could go on a quieter date next weekend. What do you think?"

Crap. What did I think? I didn't want to commit to anything so I said, "Quieter works for me. Good night, Trey."

"Night."

I exited the car and reflected on my strange evening. Trey was a great guy. I just wasn't sure if he was the guy for me.

Chapter Thirty-Six

Matt

Sunday morning, I wanted to talk to Lisa. I'd heard she'd gone on a date with Trey. I needed to know how it went. I couldn't let her know it bothered me, so I texted her. "Want to take Harry to the park?"

"When?"

I called her. "What time works for you?"

"Why don't you come over in about an hour?" She sounded like her normal self.

"See you then." There we go. Nice, short, non-stalkerish conversation. I'd see her. We would have fun. I could figure out what the hell happened between her and Trey. He might have good hair and cool clothes, but he wasn't the right fit for her. I knew that. I just had to make her see it, too.

When I knocked on her door, Harry barked like crazy. Her mom opened the door and Harry stopped barking when he saw me. Instead he wiggled all over and ran to greet me. "Hey there, buddy." I squatted down and picked him up. He licked my face and then barked to be set down.

"Lisa will be out in a minute," her mom said. "In the meantime, you can play with Harry while I finish up the breakfast dishes."

"Sure. Where's your toy, Harry?"

"*Woof.*" He ran over, grabbed his stuffed hot dog toy, and brought it to me. I picked it up and tossed it into the kitchen. He ran, skidding on the hardwood floor as he tackled the hot dog, pouncing on it, making sure it was dead. Then he brought it back and dropped it at my feet. "Who's a good dog?" I threw the toy again.

"He never gets tired of that game," Lisa said as she came down the hall.

She'd pulled her hair back off her face in a ponytail, and she wasn't wearing any makeup, but she looked amazing. "You look great," I said without really thinking about it.

"I do?" She seemed puzzled.

I threw the dog toy one more time and then walked over to greet her. I pulled her back down the hall a little bit so her mom couldn't accidentally see us. And I kissed her. She froze for a second and then she kissed me back.

When the kiss ended, she said, "What was that for?"

"I missed you yesterday, and you look really good today."

She smiled. "Thank you."

Thunder crashed outside. And then it sounded like the sky opened up as rain pounded against the roof.

"*Umm*...I don't think we're going for a walk," Lisa said.

"I'm good with that." I leaned in and kissed her again.

"*Aroo roo roo.*" The strange howling sound froze both Lisa and I mid-kiss. We turned to look at Harry who had his feet on the windowsill. It looked like his fur was sticking out more than usual and he was stiff legged like his entire body was on high alert.

"Is he barking at the storm?" Lisa asked.

"I don't know. It looks like he's saying, 'I'm not afraid of you.'"

"Harry," Lisa said. "Come here."

He took his paws off the windowsill and came to sit in front of her, tilting his head like he was confused. "What are you doing?" she asked.

Crash. Boom. Thunder shook the house.

Harry spun in a circle, barking like he was trying to figure out who was attacking us.

"Harry." I squatted down. "It's a storm." He sat but looked up at the roof with suspicion like it might attack us again at any moment.

"Maybe we should take him into the basement," Lisa said.

That worked for me for several reasons. I scooped Harry up and carried him like a football. "Come on, little guy. You can protect us from any basement monsters."

Once we were settled on the couch, Lisa started the third Harry Potter movie. Harry the dog hopped off the couch onto the coffee table. He paced back and forth, eyeing the ceiling with deep distrust.

"Is that normal dog behavior?" Lisa asked.

"I think he believes he's protecting you from the evil noises attacking the house. You have to love the spirit of small dogs. They are ready to take on the world for their humans."

"So he thinks I belong to him?"

I nodded. "Chevy and Ford work very hard to protect us from rabid squirrels and damn birds."

"Oh really?" Lisa laughed.

"Yes. When they are chasing the birds away from the greenhouse, they are very serious about it. One day my mom asked what they were barking at, and my dad said, "They're barking at the damn birds." So now all birds are damn birds."

"Your family sounds nice," she said. "Sometimes I wish I had a brother or a sister."

"I don't think they'd fit in this house," I teased.

"Shows what you know. We have a third bedroom upstairs," she said.

"Where?" The house barely seemed big enough for two. "It's tiny, even for us. A twin bed would barely fit in there. I mean it might, but there wouldn't be any space to walk around it, so we use it as storage."

"If you can't walk into the room, I don't think it counts."

"A baby crib would fit," she said.

"Do you think your mom and Tony are going to get married and have a baby?"

"I don't know. They say they might move in together once I'm in college."

The noise from the storm faded and Harry hopped off the table and came to lie next to me on the couch. He looked at me, gave a low wag, turned in a circle, and lay down.

"His work here is done," I said.

"Back to our regularly scheduled movie," Lisa said, hitting the button to start the movie.

I put my arm around her shoulders and waited to see what I should do next. It was killing me not to ask her about Trey, but it's not like I wanted to hear her say good things about the guy.

Out of the corner of my eye, I could see Lisa watching the movie. If she was comfortable with this then that was a good thing. Right? It meant she still wanted to be around me. At least I hoped so.

Chapter Thirty-Seven

Lisa

I was a terrible human being. That was the only answer. I'd had fun with Trey. He was new and different and interesting but Matt felt right. Maybe this was that go with your gut thing my mom had talked about. It's not like Trey would be heartbroken if there wasn't a second date. According to Clarissa, he had groupies in art class, so he'd be fine.

Why was dating so complicated? I was beginning to think those old-fashioned arranged marriages might not have been a terrible idea.

"What's wrong?" Matt asked.

Crap. Could he tell what I was thinking? "Nothing. Why?"

"That's the same face you make when you're doing some complicated math problem."

"I have a math face?"

He nodded. "Your eyebrows come together and you tilt your head a little bit...kind of like Harry did earlier."

I laughed. "I do not look like that."

Matt looked down at his fingernails and cleared his throat. "What were you thinking about?"

"Life in general. Everything is always more complicated than you think it's going to be."

He glanced up at me. "You don't have to share if you don't want to, but how did things go last night?"

Shit. I knew he'd hear that I'd been on a date with Trey but I never expected him to ask me about it to my face. "Are you going for the awkward moment of the year award?"

"Probably," he admitted.

"Can we not do this?" I asked.

"Do what?"

"You said we weren't exclusive."

"Yeah, but the plan was you were going to go on one date and then realize you have zero interest in him. I'm trying to see how that plan is going."

"Funny," I said. "How about we just enjoy the movie and avoid thinking big thoughts?"

He removed his arm from my shoulders. "I'm trying to be cool with this, but I think I need to leave."

"Seriously?"

He scooted away from me. "Yeah, the ball is in your court. You decide what you want and let me know." With that he stood up to leave.

"Wait." I reached for his hand.

"Why?" he asked. "Have you made a decision?"

What was with the sudden pressure? "I want you to stay. Isn't that enough?"

"Maybe it should be, but it's not."

"That's not fair," I said.

"I figured out what I want. Now it's your turn." He headed for the stairs.

This was totally sucking and it was pissing me off. "I liked you for weeks and I waited and waited, hoping something might happen, and when it didn't, I adjusted. A few months into our friendship you pull this reversal and I'm supposed to be ready for an exclusive relationship because you are? You can't even give me a few days to figure out what I want? How is that fair?"

Without turning around, he said, "All's fair in love and war." And then he headed up the steps.

Did he just say he loved me? If he had it was the worst declaration of love ever. I plopped back down on the couch and called Nina. "Can you come over and bring Oreos?"

"Is this a Double Stuf emergency or will regular do?"

"Why would anyone eat regular when Double Stuf exists?"

"Give me fifteen minutes."

By the time Nina showed up, my stomach was in knots.

I told her about Matt walking out on me.

"That's pretty ballsy. How can he expect you to make a snap decision when he dragged his feet for months?"

"I know. And what's really pissing me off is I was leaning toward choosing him."

"Really?"

"Trey is fun, but I'm not sure we like the same things."

Nina pointed at the Harry Potter movie which was still paused on the television. "You know Matt only watches those to make you happy."

"Whose side are you on?" I took two Oreos apart and smashed the double stuffed sides together. "Quadruple stuffed for when guys make you crazy."

"That looks awesome." She followed my lead, smooshing two Oreos together. She took a bite and smiled. "Yeah, that's pretty good."

"So back to Matt and Trey. I like Trey. He's fun. Matt feels like he's already part of my life. Does that make sense?"

"Kind of," she said. "So what do you want to do?"

"Would I be sucking down Double Stuf Oreos if I knew the answer to that?"

After Nina left, I went upstairs and filled my mom in. "Feel free to put on your professional counseling hat," I said. "Because I'm thoroughly confused."

"If Matt hadn't been pushy today, would you have chosen him?"

"I think so, but now I'm ticked off."

"I'm sure it wasn't easy for him to know you went on a date with Trey. He still shouldn't have walked off. Ultimatums rarely result in the desired outcome."

"Is that therapy speak for I'm right and he's wrong?"

"As a counselor I try not to assign blame, but as your mom, that was pretty immature of him to run away."

And that's when it hit me. "Oh my God. That's what he does. He never tries too hard at anything so he doesn't risk failing. He got mad at me once when I pointed that out to him. He's smart, he could make good grades, but he only works hard enough for C's. He's trying to get Charlie to go to college so he can stay home and work with his dad because I think he's afraid he won't be able to cut it in college." It felt like I'd had some kind of epiphany, but I wasn't sure what that meant for our relationship or lack thereof.

"Speaking of college," my mom said. "I know you're all set to go to Canton Community College. I also know you chose it because it was the least expensive option and you could still live at home."

I shrugged. "Since I don't really know what I want to do, it makes sense to take my general education classes there and then transfer my credits once I know what I want to do with my life." It wasn't a glamorous plan, but it worked for me.

"I think you could widen your college search if you wanted to. We'll probably never see Gavin again, and I'd prefer if we didn't, but he did make a sizable donation to your college fund."

"To ease his conscience."

"That's completely true, but it's nice that I might have finally gotten some good out of all that stress and heartache."

"Do you still want to run him over with a scooter?" I don't think I'd ever be okay with what he'd done. I was pretty sure my mom wouldn't be, either.

"I think a motorcycle would be more satisfying," she said.

I laughed.

"Remember, you don't have to make any decisions about who you want to date or what school you want to attend right now. And even if you make a decision, you are allowed to change your mind. You need to figure out what's right for you."

I had no freaking clue how to do that. "Why did you pick Tony?"

She sighed and smiled, like she was remembering something. "I used to see him jogging every day on my way to work. And I never imagined a guy in such good shape would be interested in me. I stopped at a red light one day and he was waiting for the walk sign so he could jog across the street. He noticed me looking at him and he smiled. It was a genuine smile. Like he was just being friendly. I smiled back. Over the next week we ended up at that same light three times. On the third time, he walked over and knocked on the passenger side window.

"I lowered the window and he said, 'It's hard timing my run to hit this light so I can see you every morning. Maybe we could have coffee instead.'"

"Awwww. You never told me that."

She blushed. "It kind of went against the don't talk to strangers rule I was trying to teach you."

"That's such a cute story." I pouted. "I want a guy who is going to make an effort like that for me. Matt fell ass backward into liking me. The only effort he's put into doing anything for me is giving me that Hermione wand pen."

"He wouldn't be upset if he didn't really like you," my mom said. "Give him a chance to get his head on straight. In the meantime, you can get to know Trey better."

A funny thought hit me. "Trey could be dating other people, too."

"Yes he could. Does that make you feel better?"

"Yes."

Chapter Thirty-Eight

Matt

"How could you be so stupid?" Haley demanded as I paced back and forth in front of the living room television.

"Thanks. That's helpful." I hadn't told her about what I'd said to Lisa so she could bitch at me.

"She asked for time and you gave her an ultimatum instead? No one likes those."

"It's not like I planned it." I ran my hand down my face. "Thinking of her with Trey makes me want to punch someone...preferably Trey."

"He's actually a nice guy," Haley said.

"Are you trying to piss me off?" So far she'd been less than helpful.

"You asked for my opinion," she reminded me.

"It must have been a moment of insanity," I muttered as I headed out the front door for some fresh air.

My dad sat outside on the porch swing, drinking a cup of coffee. "There's some rock that needs shoveling if you want something to take your mind off your troubles."

Not a bad idea. Sometimes physical work and being outside made me less angry. I went back inside and changed into some worn-out jeans and an old sweatshirt before heading to the area behind the greenhouse where the delivery truck had dumped landscaping rock. We moved it as we needed it up front to the wire bins. I grabbed a wheelbarrow and a shovel and got to work.

The shovel made a satisfying crunch as it bit into the waist-high pile of rock. I filled the wheelbarrow one shovelful at a time and then took it up front and dumped it in the bin. The rhythm of it relaxed me. I let my mind wander. What was I going to do about Lisa? There wasn't much I could do, except wait and see. Maybe that's what bugged me. I'd figured out what I wanted and she didn't feel the same.

Wait. That wasn't true. Like my annoying sister pointed out, I shouldn't have walked off. But I had. Now what? How did I apologize without coming off like a jerk?

With any other girl I would have given up and walked away. No one else had ever seemed worth the trouble. With Lisa, I didn't want to give up. I wanted to fight for her but I needed to find a way to do that without being a tool. How could I show her I was done running away?

I'd never given her the Harry Potter bag I'd bought for her. Maybe she wouldn't be so ticked off at me if she liked the gift. Not like I thought I could buy her affection, but I needed all the help I could get right now and it would show I understood and appreciated her nerd-girl personality.

I hated the idea of not talking to her until tomorrow.

Would she even talk to me? Maybe I should text her. Then again she wanted space. I filled and transported two more wheelbarrows of rock before I gave up on finding any answers.

All I wanted now was a shower and food. By the time I made it to the dinner table, Charlie was frowning, Haley was glaring at everyone, and my parents looked like they didn't have a clue what was going on.

I'd barely sat down and taken a bite of my burrito when Haley said, "It's stupid to be mad at Clarissa. She can't control what her cousin does."

"What if Clarissa's cousin was a girl who'd asked your boyfriend out?" Charlie said.

"That would be different," Haley said, "because Bryce is already my boyfriend."

"I appreciate the support," I said to Charlie, "but I'm the idiot who got myself into this position so there's no reason to be mad at Clarissa."

"That's surprisingly rational," Haley said.

I wanted to flip her off, but my mom would freak out, so I just ignored her comment.

"What's going on with you and Lisa?" my mom asked.

"Bad timing," I said. "She liked me. I friend-zoned her. We dated. I wasn't sure how much I liked her. Now I know that I want to date only her. She likes me but she also likes this asshat named Trey who has stupid hair."

"Nice description," Haley said.

"I was going for the G-rated version."

"How much rock did you move?" my dad asked, changing the subject.

"Three wheelbarrows."

"Why do you think Lisa is the girl you want to date?" my mom asked.

So much for eating in peace. I took another bite while I thought about why I wanted to be with her. "She's smart and she makes me laugh. I'd rather be with her than anyone else. She'll never believe that because of her asshole of a dad."

"Language," my mom said.

"He ran out on her mom when he found out she was pregnant. Asshole is the nicest description I can think of."

"You're not wrong," my dad said.

"If you really care for her, you'll find a way to make it work," my mom said.

"I'm trying."

"You really are trying, aren't you?" Haley said. "That's impressive given your dating history."

"Thanks."

"Topic change," she said. "Jane talked Nathan into asking his dad to donate money to the shelter so we can build a dog washing station."

"What's a dog washing station?" I asked. "And don't tell me it's a station where you wash dogs."

She grinned. "It's like an outdoor shower with six stalls. So we can keep the dogs clean, which should make them seem more adoptable."

"That's cool," I said. "Nathan seems like a decent guy."

"He is."

"Your boyfriend on the other hand..."

She stuck her tongue out at me, which made all of us laugh. The strange tension was gone.

After dinner, I sat on my bed, staring at the piss-poor essay I'd written for Geography when Charlie came into our room.

"You and Clarissa okay?" I asked.

"Yeah, I guess. Have you figured out how you're going to straighten things out with Lisa?"

"No. So far my brilliant plan is to give her the Harry Potter stuff I bought her."

Charlie stared at the bag where it sat on my dresser.

"Didn't you say Trey wasn't into that kind of stuff?"

"I don't think he is."

"Then maybe you should make sure he sees Lisa being all happy about it."

"Let him see her in full fangirl mode?"

"He *is* the too cool for school guy," Charlie said. "He probably thinks Harry Potter is a kids' movie."

Could I do it? Lisa claimed I always sabotaged myself. What if the only way to get what I wanted was to sabotage her?

Chapter Thirty-Nine

Lisa

Monday morning, I woke up to find my mom was way too happy. She was dressed and in full makeup before I'd even eaten breakfast. "Who are you and what have you done with my mother?"

"I'm meeting Tony for breakfast this morning. It's the anniversary of when he knocked on my car window."

"Oh...that's so sweet."

"I think so." She grabbed her purse. "I'll see you tonight for dinner."

"Have fun." I liked seeing her happy. It gave me hope that I might find a guy who wasn't a tool. My cell buzzed with a text. Speaking of tools, it was from Matt.

"Sorry I bailed. You can have all the time you need. Let me know when you decide. I have a nerd-girl suck-up gift as a peace offering. I'll see you at your locker."

Now what? Did I text back? Did I let him sweat it out? He'd been a tool, but he was recognizing that fact. Not sure what to say, I texted back a smiley face.

On the drive to school, I tried to imagine my life without Trey. That wasn't hard to do. Imagining my life without Matt was a lot harder. Did that mean he was the one for me or that our lives were intertwined due to our friends? Better question...how would I feel if I saw Matt with another girl? The idea of him with Jane irritated the crap out of me. What about someone else? What if Clarissa fixed him up with one of her friends and I had to watch him holding hands and doing other romantic things with someone else? Acid surged in my stomach. Either I'd had too much orange juice at breakfast or I didn't want to see him with someone else. Where did that leave me?

I pulled into a space in the parking lot and stared at my steering wheel like it might have some answers to my current conundrum. It did not. Darn it. I'd just go face Matt and see what happened. I'd barely climbed out of my car when Trey appeared out of thin air.

"No yelling at the universe this morning?" he asked.

Uh-oh. I'd spent so much time worried about what I'd say to Matt that I forgot to think about what I'd say to Trey.

"That's not a happy face," he said.

"Sorry. My brain isn't up to full speed yet." I headed toward the sidewalk and he fell into step beside me.

"I'm not really a morning person, either," he said. "Today feels like it's going to be a good day."

Damn it. Should I say something? Was I obligated to respond? I faked a yawn...which turned into a real yawn. "Sorry. I need about two more hours of sleep."

"No problem." When we entered the building I hoped he'd head for his locker, wherever that was, but he stayed by my side like he was walking me to my locker which was not a good idea. When we were about a hundred feet from my destination, I said, "Matt asked to meet me at my locker, so..."

"So you don't want me to come with you?" he said, like he thought it was a joke.

"It could be a little awkward." I could see Matt up ahead, but he hadn't spotted me yet. "I'll see you later, okay?"

"I'll just wait across the hall."

That was not what I wanted, but it would have to do. As Trey veered left, Matt spotted me and smiled. Good. He must not have seen me with Trey. And now I was nervous. When I reached my locker, he said, "This is an I was an idiot and I promise not to run away when things get complicated gift."

The shopping bag was from the bookstore. That was a good start. I opened it up and sucked in a breath. It was the Platform 9 ¾ mailbag I'd wanted. "Oh my gosh. I tried to buy this but they were sold out."

"Open it."

I unbuckled the flap. Inside was a Gryffindor notebook and two pairs of Harry Potter socks.

"I didn't remember seeing you wear those, so I hope you don't have them."

He'd paid attention to my socks. "I don't." Why did it feel like I was going to cry? He really got me. "Thank you."

The bell for homeroom was going to ring in about five minutes and I didn't know what to do.

"Is it your birthday and you didn't tell me?" Trey asked as he came over to join us. He saw what I was holding and said, "Wait. No. That must be a joke gift."

"Why do you say that?" I asked.

"Oh." He seemed to realize he'd made a mistake. "You're into that kind of stuff? I thought Harry Potter was for kids."

"It's a nerd-girl thing," Matt said.

Trey glanced up at Matt and then at me. "You're okay with him calling you a nerd?"

I nodded. "That's who I am. I like Harry Potter and Doctor Who."

He backed up a step. "And you'd rather read than talk to people and go listen to loud music."

I nodded.

"I like you, but I don't think we're into the same things. Maybe we're better off as friends."

"Probably," I said. That went way easier than I thought it would.

"See you around." Trey walked off and I didn't have to feel guilty. Things were finally falling into place.

I glanced over at Matt. He was smiling...not like he was happy, like he'd somehow won. I mean he had, in a way, but something about this situation was off. I looked down at the Harry Potter bag I was holding. Wait a minute. "Did you set me up?"

"What are you talking about?"

"You set me up. You knew I'd go all nerd-girl over this stuff and then Trey wouldn't be interested in me anymore."

"I bought these for you a week ago. How would I know that?"

My life had gone from happy to crappy in thirty seconds. "Don't lie to me."

He took a deep breath and blew it out. "I'm not lying. I bought this for you the day you were upset about Jane. And I confessed to Jane that I used to have a crush on her so you don't have to worry about that anymore. I bought you this to show you I understand you and I like you for *you*."

Everything he said seemed heartfelt but there was still one problem. "What about Trey?"

"I knew he probably wouldn't understand your nerdy side and I hoped that might work out in my favor."

The bell for homeroom rang. I turned around and walked off. It felt like I was drowning in a rising tide of confusion. On the one hand, Matt understood me and liked me for who I was. *Woo-hoo!* On the other hand, he'd set me up and I didn't like being manipulated.

In between classes I griped to Nina. "If he'd let me make my own mind up, it would have worked out in his favor. Why did he have to do that?"

"Well...he gets marks for being inventive. He trapped you in a web of your own nerdiness."

"I know."

"And you wanted someone to fight for you. In his slightly sneaky way, he did that."

She was right. By lunch I wasn't mad so much as disappointed and irritated. I needed to know I could trust Matt. I needed him to be honest with me. When he sat down next to me and opened his mouth like he was going to argue his case, I stopped him.

"Please don't talk. Just listen."

"Has she gone off the deep end?" West said to Nina.

I glared at him. "Do you want to see me go off the deep end?"

"*Umm*...no."

"Then butt out." I turned back to Matt. "Just so you know, I was going to pick you. If you hadn't set me up, we'd both be happy right now." I waited. He raised his eyebrows at me. Oh right. "Now you should talk."

"I fought dirty because the idea of you with another guy makes me crazy. You're it for me. And I'm going to keep apologizing until you forgive me."

"That sounds annoying."

"If you accept my apology we could move past the annoying part."

At the end of the day, I headed to Crazy Crafts for my Monday Mask workshop.

Three girls were making masks. Two wanted fairies and one wanted to be a dragon. "Works for me," I said.

We glued on ribbons and sequins and feathers until the girls were happy with their masks. We had a snack that one of their moms had provided...apple slices, which was a good thing because at this point I'd eaten way too many

Oreos. After all the girls had been signed out, I straightened up the yarn section, putting wayward skeins of yarn back into the correct bins. Busywork occupied my mind until it was time to clock out.

On the way home, my conscience ate at me. I should call Matt. He was a good guy. He hadn't done anything terrible. He'd proven to me what he'd said all along. Trey and I weren't into the same things. Though, I wish he would've let things run their natural course rather than prodding them along.

When I pulled up to my house, I didn't recognize it. There were flowers everywhere. Terra-cotta pots with miniature rose bushes sat next to planters full of tulips and lilies. There were pink, red, purple, and white flowers I didn't recognize overflowing in plastic pots. It looked like someone had turned my front yard into a flower shop. When I climbed out of my car, their scent drifted through the air. My mom opened the front door and smiled at me. She held out a card. "This is for you."

I walked up the steps and grabbed the card. I knew this was Matt's doing. I opened the card.

Because I should have given you flowers a long time ago. Love, Matt.

Awwww. That was so sweet...and clever.

"He's good," my mom said. "He must really like you because he promised to plant these wherever we wanted *and* to take care of the yard from now on."

That was a commitment. Not the sign of a guy who planned to bail when things became tough.

"You should go see the backyard," she said.

"There's more?" I entered the house. Harry ran over to me, wiggling with joy. "Hey, buddy." I picked him up and headed into the kitchen and out the sliding glass doors. Matt sat at the patio table. He had six bags of Double Stuf Oreos stacked up with a wide red ribbon tied around them like they were a present.

"Is that your backup in case I didn't like the flowers?"

"Maybe," he said, like he wasn't sure. "Do you like the flowers?"

I nodded and set Harry down before joining Matt at the table. He gave me another card.

The Oreos are for when I do things that tick you off, which I'll try to avoid, if at all possible, but you know how that will probably work out. And, if you're still undecided, remember I gave you a dog. Love, Matt

He reached over and laced his fingers through mine. "I did give you a dog."

"You did."

"And I read in the how to date like a normal guy book that accepting a dog means you're officially boyfriend and girlfriend."

"It does? I don't remember seeing that in my book," I said.

"Maybe you should read it again," he said. "Here." He handed me a notebook.

On the front in black sharpie it said, *How to date a nerd-girl and keep her happy.* I flipped it open and inside it said:

1. *Give her a dog.*
2. *Watch Harry Potter movies.*
3. *Keep Double Stuf Oreos on hand in case of emergencies.*
4. *Give her flowers.*

5. *Keep track of which Harry Potter socks she has so you can find new ones she needs.*

6. *Hang around and annoy her until she agrees that she's your girlfriend.*

"Who am I to argue with a book?" I leaned in to kiss him. He may not always be perfect, but he was perfect for me.

Epilogue

Lisa

"Is triple dating even a thing?" Matt asked as we walked into The Slicery with Charlie and Clarissa.

"Doesn't matter," I said, "because apparently it's what we're doing." I waved to Nina as we walked across the restaurant to meet her and West.

"I didn't realize Nina was so pushy," Clarissa said. "Not that I don't want to hang out with you guys, but geez."

"She's just enthusiastic." Actually, this had been my idea because I was worried the whole dating Trey thing might have messed up Charlie and Clarissa's relationship. I didn't want to be responsible for that, so I shared my plan with Nina and she agreed to pretend it was her idea to make it all a little less awkward. Plus she was known to argue her point until people caved which is exactly what she'd done with Clarissa. The ends justified the means.

When we reached the table, Nina and West were pointing at the menu and debating what we should order. "It would make more sense for us to order two extra-large pizzas," West said.

Nina sighed. "That would work, but you like mushrooms and Lisa won't touch them. She'll insist on meatball pizza which you don't like and I have no idea what Clarissa and Charlie will want." She and West both looked at Clarissa.

"What's your pizza preference?" Nina asked.

"Why does it feel like I'm taking a test?" Clarissa asked as she sat down.

"Don't worry," I said as I settled into my chair. "There's no wrong answer except pineapple."

"Okay." Clarissa pushed the menu away. "This will probably throw off your whole equation, but I like plain cheese pizza."

"Just cheese?" I wasn't adventurous in my eating, but that seemed a little boring.

"We usually split a half cheese and half bacon pepperoni pizza," Charlie said.

"Three pizzas it is," Nina said.

"Or four," Matt said. "Because bacon pepperoni is pretty awesome."

"So that's one sausage mushroom, one meatball, one bacon pepperoni and one cheese?" Nina said.

"How can we need four pizzas for three couples?" West asked.

"Doesn't matter," I said. "It's what we're doing to keep everyone happy. Plus there will be leftovers to take home. Cold meatball pizza is one of my favorite breakfasts."

Matt grimaced. "That's just wrong."

"You can stick with your Cap'n Crunch," I said. "Cold pizza makes me happy."

"Speaking of things that make you happy..." Matt leaned in and pressed his lips against mine. My heart tripped a beat as I kissed him back. When the kiss ended he sat back and smiled at me.

It still didn't seem real sometimes that Matt and I were together...officially a couple. It had been a few weeks now and so far things were working for us. There had been a few bumps in the road...I was still a little jealous of Jane because she was a cute bouncy blonde while I was a normal nerdy brunette, but Matt didn't seem to notice her as much as I did. Either he was acting like he didn't notice her because he was into me, or he really was that into me.

And I needed to trust him because he'd kept his word so far. He'd planted all the flowers and came over to mow the lawn every weekend. He'd even painted a set of Harry Potter book bricks for me.

"Time for me to confess something," Matt said. "Okay." I had no idea what he was going to say, but I trusted it wouldn't be too awful.

"I signed up for some business classes at Canton."

"You did? That's great." I was going to Canton Community College because I still wasn't sure what I wanted to do with my life and there was no reason to spend money my mom didn't have before I figured that out. Thanks to the sperm donor I had cash for a more prestigious school. Once I knew what I wanted to be when I grew up, I might dip into his donation. Until then, I'd spend time with Matt and enjoy figuring my life out. I'd gone from the friend zone to a fake relationship and then ended up in a real relationship, which kind of gave a whole new meaning to the phrase *fake it until you make it.*

Also by Chris Cannon

Going Down In Flames Series

Going Down In Flames

Bridges Burned

Trial By Fire

Fanning The Flames

Burning Bright

Mysteries of Mystic Hills

Murder in Mystic Hills

Double Trouble in Mystic Hills

SpellBound in Mystic Hills

Sweet Snarky Romance Series

The Boyfriend Bet

Boomerang Boyfriend: Best Friend's Brother

Romance

The Dating Debate

99% Faking It

Watch for more at www.chriscannonauthor.com

Don't miss out!

Visit the website below and you can sign up to receive emails whenever Chris Cannon publishes a new book. There's no charge and no obligation.

https://books2read.com/r/B-A-EDWG-ILMOD

BOOKS 2 READ

Connecting independent readers to independent writers.

Also by Chris Cannon

Going Down In Flames
Bridges Burned
Trial By Fire
Fanning The Flames
Burning Bright

Mysteries of Mystic Hills
Murder in Mystic Hills
Double Trouble in Mystic Hills
SpellBound in Mystic Hills

Sweet Snarky Romance Series
The Boyfriend Bet
Boomerang Boyfriend
The Dating Debate
99% Faking It

Watch for more at https://www.chriscannonauthor.com/.

www.ingramcontent.com/pod-product-compliance
Lightning Source LLC
Chambersburg PA
CBHW020433180626
46812CB00003B/1204